Scott Hudson's High School Survival Tips

★ Keep away from seniors.

★ Keep away from juniors.

★ It's probably a good idea to avoid sophomores, too, since most of them seem to want revenge for what happened when they were freshmen.

★ Don't ever kneel. Especially if there are big kids around.

★ Never wear a dorky hat. Especially if there are big kids around.

★ Don't carry your books under your arm in a crowded hall.

★ Try to avoid the bus, even if it means catching a ride from a stranger with a chain saw.

★ If you're friends with a girl in kindergarten, try to stay friends with her when you get older because otherwise she might forget she ever knew you, and she might get so drop-dead gorgeous you don't have the guts to remind her that you once shared a pack of peanut-butter crackers.

★ If you're going to break something, a nose is probably better than an arm, since it heals faster and it makes you look tough.

OTHER BOOKS YOU MAY ENJOY

Sleeping freshmen { never lie }

DAVID LUBAR

speak
An Imprint of Penguin Group (USA) Inc.

SPEAK
Published by the Penguin Group
Penguin Group (USA) Inc.,
345 Hudson Street, New York, New York 10014, U.S.A.
Penguin Group (Canada), 90 Eglinton Avenue East, Suite 700,
Toronto, Ontario, Canada M4P 2Y3 (a division of Pearson Penguin Canada Inc.)
Penguin Books Ltd, 80 Strand, London WC2R 0RL, England
Penguin Ireland, 25 St Stephen's Green, Dublin 2, Ireland
(a division of Penguin Books Ltd)
Penguin Group (Australia), 250 Camberwell Road, Camberwell, Victoria 3124, Australia
(a division of Pearson Australia Group Pty Ltd)
Penguin Books India Pvt Ltd, 11 Community Centre,
Panchsheel Park, New Delhi - 110 017, India
Penguin Group (NZ), Cnr Airborne and Rosedale Roads,
Albany, Auckland 1310, New Zealand (a division of Pearson New Zealand Ltd)
Penguin Books (South Africa) (Pty) Ltd, 24 Sturdee Avenue, Rosebank,
Johannesburg 2196, South Africa

Registered Offices: Penguin Books Ltd, 80 Strand, London WC2R 0RL, England

First published in the United States of America by Dutton Children's Books,
a division of Penguin Young Readers Group, 2005
Published by Speak, an imprint of Penguin Group (USA) Inc., 2007

5 7 9 10 8 6

Copyright © David Lubar, 2005
All rights reserved

THE LIBRARY OF CONGRESS HAS CATALOGED
THE DUTTON CHILDREN'S BOOKS EDITION AS FOLLOWS:
Lubar, David.
Sleeping freshmen never lie / by David Lubar.—1st ed.
p.   cm.
Summary: While navigating his first year of high school and awaiting the birth of his new
baby brother, Scott loses old friends and gains some unlikely new ones as he hones his skills
as a writer.
ISBN: 0-525-47311-4 (hc)
[1. Self-confidence—Fiction. 2. Conduct of life—Fiction. 3. Interpersonal relations—
Fiction. 4. Authorship—Fiction. 5. Brothers—Fiction. 6. High schools—Fiction.
7. Schools—Fiction. 8. Pennsylvania—Fiction.] I. Title.
PZ7.L96775S1 2005
[Fic]—dc22 2004023067

Speak ISBN 978-0-14-240780-6

Designed by R. Lawrence Amari

Printed in the United States of America

For Walter Mayes,
a giant not just in size, but in heart and mind

ACKNOWLEDGMENTS

My deepest thanks to Michele Coppola, who edited this book through three vastly different versions and talked me out of my foolhardy attempt to do the whole thing the wrong way; to Stephanie Owens Lurie, for taking a risk or two; to Doug Baldwin and Heather Baldwin, for honest and valuable feedback; to Andrea Mosbacher and Martin Karlow, for gentle and accurate copyediting; and to all those brilliant folks who tried to help me in the elusive hunt for the perfect title. And, oh yeah, thanks to my family, my cats, everyone who knows it's okay to laugh while reading, and to all the good English teachers out there.

Sleeping freshmen **never lie**

{ **one** }

We plunged toward the future without a clue. Tonight, we were four sweaty guys heading home from a day spent shooting hoops. Tomorrow, I couldn't even guess what would happen. All I knew for sure was that our lives were about to change.

"Any idea what it'll be like?" I asked. My mind kept flashing images of cattle. They shuffled up a ramp, unaware that their path led to a slaughterhouse.

"A *Tomb Raider* movie," Patrick said. "Or *Indiana Jones.*"

"It'll be the same as always," Kyle said. "Boring and stupid."

Patrick shook his head. "Nope. *Tomb Raider,* for sure. We'll get eaten alive if we aren't careful, but we'll be surrounded by amazing stuff."

"Right. Amazing stuff," Mitch said. He rubbed his hands together as if he were about to dive into a juicy burger. "High school girls. Hundreds of 'em."

"Like we have a chance with them," Patrick said. "I heard the seniors snag all the hot girls."

"Not when I'm around." Kyle slicked his hair back with his right hand, then made a fist and flexed his biceps. "Girls melt when I get near them."

"Mostly from the fumes," Patrick said.

"What about the classes?" I asked as Kyle shoved Patrick toward the curb. "Think they'll be hard?"

"Who cares?" Mitch said. "You just have to show up and you'll pass."

We reached my house. Second from the corner on Willow Street. The guys lived on the other side of the neighborhood. I realized that the next time we saw one another, we'd be freshmen at J. P. Zenger High.

Freshmen. Unbelievable. Fresh? Definitely. Men? Not a clue. I turned toward my friends.

"Bye," Patrick said.

Mitch grunted a farewell. Kyle's hand twitched in a lazy wave. I wanted to say something more meaningful than *See ya later.*

There they were, right in front of me—Kyle, who I'd known since kindergarten, Patrick, who I'd met in second grade, and Mitch, who'd moved here in sixth grade. We'd done everything together, all through middle school. The perfect words were so obvious, I couldn't help smiling as I spoke. "One for all and all for one."

The phrase was greeted with silence. Around us, I could hear the last crickets of summer chirping faintly. The crickets, too, seemed puzzled.

"One for all . . ." I said again.

Mitch frowned. "One for all what?"

"Is that like a Marines slogan?" Kyle asked.

"No, I think it's on coins. It's that Latin stuff, right?" Patrick said. "It's *E Pluto Pup* something or other."

"It's from *The Three Musketeers*," I told them. "It's a famous book."

Three pairs of eyes stared at me without a glimmer.

"There's a movie, too," I said. "These guys stuck together no matter what."

Kyle looked around, tapped his thumb against the tip of each of his fingers, then said, "But there are four of us."

"Absolutely. That's what's so perfect. There were four Musketeers, too."

"That's stupid," Mitch said. "Somebody couldn't count."

"Well, anyhow, let's stick together tomorrow," I said.

"You bet," Patrick said.

"For sure," Mitch said.

"One for all and all for me," Kyle said. He turned to go.

"See ya later," I called as they walked off.

Mom and Dad were side by side on the living-room couch. The TV was on, but it didn't look like they were watching it. They stopped talking when I walked in.

"What's up?" I asked.

"Hi, Scott," Dad said. "You have fun with your friends?"

"Yeah." I noticed his eyes kept shifting from me to Mom. "Is something going on?"

"Tomorrow's the big day," Mom said. "You must be excited."

Now I got it. They were stressed out from worrying whether they were headed for another disaster, which was one of the milder ways to describe my brother Bobby's high school experience.

"I'm sure I'll do fine." I could almost guarantee I wouldn't skip history seventeen straight days in a row, get nabbed nine times for public displays of affection—with nine different girls—or pull off any of the other stunts that helped end Bobby's high school experience half a year earlier than planned. "I'm really excited about school."

"Good." Mom smiled with way more joy than the situation seemed to call for. "Do you want me to make you a lunch? I bought your favorite rolls."

"No." I tried to hide my shudder as I imagined carrying a paper bag into the cafeteria. "Thanks."

"I think he'd rather buy lunch," Dad said.

I nodded, shot Dad a grateful look, and headed upstairs. I wanted to get my stuff ready, and they probably wanted to talk more about how there was nothing to worry about because I was different from Bobby.

Man, was that ever true. Bobby was almost as tall as Dad, good with tools, and strong enough to carry two sacks of concrete at once. Eighty pounds on one shoulder. That sort of load would snap my spine. Girls chased him like he was some kind of movie star. He'd gotten all the good genes. I was a runt who had to think hard to remember which way to turn a wrench.

I put my stuff in my backpack. Then I grabbed the books I'd bought last Saturday. Dad and I had gone to the flea market up near Stroudsburg. We go there at least once a month when it's open. He looks for tools. I look for books. I'd snagged a whole stack of Robert Heinlein novels for two bucks, and a *Field Guide to North American Game Fish* for fifty cents. Dad had gotten some huge clamps for five bucks. That's the weird thing about flea markets—books and tools seem to cost about the same amount per pound.

I crammed the novels into one of my bookcases, then sat on my bed and leafed through the field guide, looking at the color photos of smallmouth bass and imagining landing a four pounder while wading in the Delaware.

Before I went to sleep, I called Bobby at his apartment to see if I could get any advice from him about school. Which I guess was like asking General Custer for combat tips. It didn't matter. He wasn't in.

That night, I dreamed I was field-testing flamethrowers for the army. In a supermarket. I awoke to the smell of bacon.

First day of high school.

I couldn't believe it was finally here. Dad had already left for work. Mom was sitting on a stool by the kitchen counter, reading a magazine. But as my nose had told me, she'd been hard at work creating breakfast. "Good morning," she said. She slipped the magazine under the newspaper. "Hungry?"

"Starved."

Mom always made blueberry pancakes and bacon on the first day of school. As she loaded up my plate with enough protein and carbs to fuel a Mars mission, I glanced at the corner of the magazine where it stuck out from under the paper. Mom didn't usually hide stuff. It was probably one of those supermarket things, with stories about aliens who looked like Elvis and kids who'd been raised in the desert by giant toads.

Mom got herself a plate and joined me as I tried to make a dent in my stack. We didn't talk much while we ate. She seemed to be a million miles away.

"You okay?" I asked.

The too-big smile reappeared. "I can still make you a lunch. There's plenty of time."

"Maybe tomorrow." I glanced at the clock. "Gotta go." I grabbed my backpack and headed for the bus stop.

I was the first one there. I should have brought a book to help kill the time. But that would immediately mark me as a real geek.

Eventually, I heard a noise in the distance. "Hey, Scottie," Mouth Kandeski shouted when he was still half a block away. "Whatcha think? High school. It's the big time. We're in high school. Man, that's cool. That's sooooo cool."

He dribbled a trail of words like a leaking milk carton as he closed the distance between us. My best guess is that he can only breathe when he's talking.

"Hi, Mouth," I said when he reached me. His name's Louden. Bad move on his parents' part. He got called Loud-mouth the moment he started school. It was shortened to Mouth soon after that. We didn't hang out or anything, but I guess since I was one of the few kids on the planet who'd never screamed, "Shut up!" at him, he figured I was interested in what he had to say. I was more interested in wondering what would happen to him if I clamped a hand over his mouth. Maybe he'd swell up and explode. Maybe the top of his head would pop off, sending his dorky orange ball cap into orbit where it belonged. Maybe the words would shoot out of his butt with so much force his pants would rip.

Left unclamped, Mouth had plenty more to discuss. "I'll tell you, I can't wait. This is awesome. I'm kinda nervous. Are you nervous? I mean, I'm not scared, or nothing, but just kinda nervous. You know, nervous isn't the same as scared. It's sort of like the buzz you get from lots of coffee. I drank eight cups, once. I started drinking coffee this summer. You drink coffee? It's not bad if you put in enough sugar."

Past Mouth, I spotted more freshmen. Familiar faces from Tom Paine Middle School, looking like Easter eggs in their new clothes. Then one unfamiliar face. A goddess. An honest-to-goodness goddess. At the first sight of her, even from a distance, I felt like I'd been stabbed in the gut with an icicle. I wanted to gather branches and build a shrine, or slay a mastodon and offer her the finest pieces, fresh from the hunt.

"Whoa, it's Julia," Mouth said, breaking the spell. "Hey, Julia, you look different."

Wow. Mouth was right. It was Julia Baskins. I'd known her most of my life, and I hadn't recognized her. She was one of those kids who blend into the background. Like me, I guess. Well, the background had lost a blender. She was gorgeous.

She'd always kept her dark brown hair in a braid. Now it was cut short and shaggy, with a couple of highlights. She was wearing makeup that did amazing things to her eyes, and a sweater and khakis that did amazing things to the rest of her. She looked taller, too.

"You're wearing contacts, right?" Mouth called to her. "I

wanted contacts, but Mom said I had to wait until I got more responsible. Just because I let my braces get gunked up and had all those cavities. And lost my retainer three times. Well, really just twice. The other time, my dog ate it, so that doesn't count. You have a dog?"

Julia shook her head and managed to squeeze in the word "Cat."

"I don't have a cat. I have an Airedale," Mouth said. "He's not purebred, but that's what we think he mostly is." He jammed his hand into his jacket pocket, fished around, and pulled out a broken Oreo. "Want a cookie?"

"No, thanks." Julia slipped away from Mouth and joined her friend Kelly Holbrook near the curb. I worked my way closer and tried to think of some excuse to talk to her.

I never got the chance.

a hush fell over our cluster of freshmen, cloaking us with that same sense of dread that ancient civilizations must have felt during a solar eclipse. But we weren't awestruck by a dragon eating the sun. We were facing a much less mythical danger.

Older kids. An army of giants. I'd just spent a year in eighth grade, towering over the sixth and seventh graders. Okay— that was an exaggeration. I only towered over the short ones. But I wasn't used to being at the bottom of the food chain. Or the wrong end of a growth spurt. I felt like the towel boy for the Sixers.

As the loud, joking, shoving mob reached us, I slipped toward the back of the group and pretended to adjust my watch. Out of the corner of my eye I noticed a kid kneel to tie his shoe. That earned him a kick in the rear from a member of the mob as it passed by.

Mouth kept talking. Big mistake. The giants closed in on him, dumped the contents of his backpack onto the sidewalk, and threw his hat down a storm drain.

"Hey, come on, guys," Mouth said as his possessions spilled

across the concrete. "Come on. Hey. Stop it. Come on, that's not funny. We're all classmates, right? We all go to the same school. Let's be friends."

The scary thing was that the big kids didn't seem angry. I'm pretty sure they trashed his stuff by reflex, like they were scratching an itch or squashing a bug. Some people step on ants. Some people step on freshmen. I guess it was better to be a freshman than an ant. At least the seniors didn't have giant magnifying glasses.

Mouth was spared from further damage by the arrival of transportation. With an ear-killing squeal of brakes, the bus skidded to the curb, bathing us in the thick aroma of diesel fuel, motor oil, and a faint whiff of cooked antifreeze. The driver opened the door and glared at Mouth as the mob pushed their way aboard. "Pick up that mess, kid!" he shouted.

When I walked past Mouth, I thought about giving him a hand.

"You're holding us up!" the driver shouted. He kept his glare aimed in my direction while he took a gulp of coffee from a grimy thermos cup. Great—of all the types of bus drivers in the world, I had to get a shouter.

I hurried on board, hoping to grab a seat near Julia. No such luck.

As dangerous as the bus stop is, at least there are places to run. There's no escape from the bus. It's like a traveling version of a war game. All that's missing is paintball guns and maybe a couple foxholes. I could swear one of the kids in the back was in his twenties. I think he was shaving.

I sat up front.

That wasn't much better, since every big kid who got on at the rest of the stops had a chance to smack my head. I should have grabbed a seat behind Sheldon Murmbower. There was something about his head that attracted swats. Everyone within two or three rows of him was pretty safe.

For the moment, all I could do was try to learn invisibility. I opened my backpack and searched for something to keep me busy. Now I really wished I'd brought that field guide, or anything else to read. All I had was blank notebooks, pens, and pencils. I grabbed a notebook. The driver was shouting at a new batch of kids as they got on. Then he shouted at Mouth, who was sitting in the front seat.

"Shut up, kid! You're distracting me."

Last year was so much better. I had the greatest driver. Louie. He used to drive a city bus. That gave me an idea. I started writing. It didn't cut down on the smacks as much as I'd hoped, but it kept my mind off them.

Scott Hudson's Field Guide to School-Bus Drivers

Retired City-Bus Driver: Unbelievably skilled. Can fit the bus through the narrowest opening. Never hits anything by accident but might bump a slow-moving car on purpose. Spits out the window a lot. Never looks in the mirror to check on us. Knows all the best swear words.

Ex-hippie (or Child of Hippies): Has a ponytail, smiles too much, uses words like *groovy*. Likes to weave back and forth between the lanes in time to Grateful Dead music.

Wears loose, colorful clothing. Smells like incense.
Refuses to believe it's the twenty-first century.
College Student: Similar to the hippie, but no ponytail.
Hits stuff once in a while. Studies for exams while
driving. Sometimes takes naps at red lights or does
homework while steering with knees.
Beginner: Very nervous. Goes slowly. Can't get out of
first gear, but still manages to hit stuff pretty often.
Makes all kinds of cool sounds when frightened.
Occasionally shuts eyes.
Shouter: Very loud. Goes fast. Slams the door. Likes
country music, NASCAR, and black coffee. Hands tend to
shake when they're not clutching the wheel. Often has
broken blood vessels in eyes. Usually needs a shave.
Always needs a shower.

Twenty minutes and one full page later, we reached J. P. Zenger High.

"No pushing," the driver shouted as we scrambled out.

"High school," Mouth said, staggering to the side as someone pushed him out of the way. "Here we come. This is going to be great. We're going to rule this place."

Wrong, Mouth. Wrong, wrong, wrong, wrong, wrong.

There were so many buses, the parking lot smelled like a truck stop. On top of that, the lot was jammed with a long line of parents dropping off kids and a wave of seniors driving their own cars with varying degrees of skill.

I stood on the curb for a moment, my eyes wide and my head tilted back. I'd seen it a thousand times before, but I'd never really looked at it. Zenger High was huge. It sprawled out like a hotel that had a desperate desire to become an octopus. Every couple years, the town built another addition. The school mascot should have been a bulldozer.

My homeroom was located as far as possible from the bus area. I got lost twice. The first time, I asked some older kid for directions, and he sent me off to what turned out to be the furnace room. I assumed this was an example of upperclassman humor. The janitor, who I'd wakened from a nap, yelled at me. I reached my desk just before the late bell rang.

I didn't see a single familiar face in homeroom. The teacher passed out blank assignment books. Then he gave us our schedules. I scanned mine, hoping to get at least a clue about what lay ahead.

Period	Class	Teacher
1st	H. English	Mr. Franka
2nd	Gym/Study Hall	Mr. Cravutto/Staff
3rd	Art	Ms. Savitch
4th	Lunch	
5th	C.P. History	Mr. Ferragamo
6th	C.P. Algebra	Ms. Flutemeyer
7th	Life Skills	Ms. Pell
8th	C.P. Spanish	Ms. de Gaulle
9th	C.P. Chemistry	Ms. Balmer

I had no idea what the *H* or the *C.P.* stood for. Since there was no teacher listed for lunch, I grabbed a pen and wrote *Mr. E. Meat.*

My first class turned out to be as far as possible from homeroom, and nearly impossible to find. But at least I knew enough not to ask for directions. Ten minutes into my freshman year, I'd already learned an important lesson.

When I reached the room, I finally saw a face I recognized. The same face I hadn't recognized earlier. Julia was in my English class, along with Kelly, and a couple other kids I knew. Still no sign of Kyle, Patrick, or Mitch.

I grabbed a seat two rows away from Julia. Things were looking up.

"Welcome to Honors English," Mr. Franka said. He was a short guy with a beard and sideburns and the sort of rugged face you see on the cable hunting shows. Instead of a camouflage outfit, he was wearing a light blue button-down shirt with the sleeves rolled up, but no tie or jacket. "I hope you all love to read." He grabbed a stack of paperbacks from his desk and started tossing them out like literary Frisbees. I noticed a Marine tattoo on his left forearm.

He also passed out a textbook, which weighed about nine pounds. Fortunately, he didn't toss it. Otherwise, there'd probably have been a death or two in the back row.

Instead of reading in class, we started discussing how to define a short story. It was actually fun. I didn't say too much. I didn't want anyone to think I was some kind of brain—which I'm not. I wasn't even sure how I'd ended up in the honors class. Maybe it was because of the tests we'd taken at the end of last year.

Mr. Franka kept asking us all sorts of questions to keep the discussion going. At one point, he said, "What do you think is easier to write, a short story or a novel?"

I almost raised my hand. I'd read so many of both, I figured I had a good answer. A story was harder because you couldn't wander around. You had to stick to the subject. At least in a good story. It was a matter of focus.

Most of the kids said that a novel would be harder because it was longer. I wasn't sure whether to speak up or just keep quiet. Then Julia raised her hand. "I think stories are harder," she said. "In a novel, the writer can wander. In a story, the writer has to stay focused."

"Right!" Oh great. I hadn't meant to shout. But it was so amazing to find we felt the same way. Everyone was looking at me. "I agree," I said in a quieter voice as I slunk down in my seat. Wonderful. Now she'd think I was some kind of suck-up.

At the end of the period, Mr. Franka wrote our homework on the board and passed out a vocabulary book. One class—three books. This was not a good sign.

There was a dash for the door when the bell rang. The hall was jammed with freshmen walking in circles, ellipses, zig-zags, and other patterns that marked us as clueless members of the lost generation. Or lost members of the clueless generation.

I saw Patrick in study hall, but the teacher wouldn't let us talk. For some reason, he thought we should be studying.

We made color charts in art class, which was pretty interesting. On the way out, Ms. Savitch gave us a photocopy of an article about Van Gogh. I was beginning to calculate my reading load by the pound instead of the page. But that was okay. I could handle it.

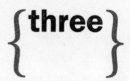

{ three }

I met up with the guys at lunch. I got there late because the cafeteria is not only really far from my art class, but also amazingly well hidden. I probably never would have found it if I hadn't detected the unique aroma of burned hair, rotting peaches, and cinnamon drifting out the door. Oh—and a subtle hint of butterscotch pudding.

"How's it going?" I asked. At least this part felt familiar. We'd sat together through middle school. Even the round tables were the same. And the wobbly plastic chairs.

"It's going fine," Kyle said.

Patrick nodded. "Yup. As long as you stay out of the way of the seniors, it's okay. Except for getting lost."

"Yeah, this place is like a tesseract," I said.

Three pairs of eyes stared at me.

"You know. A tesseract. From *A Wrinkle in Time.*"

The stares were joined by head shakes.

"A cube twisted into another dimension," I said.

Head shakes gave way to sighs. Eyes rolled toward the ceiling. Shrugging shoulders twisted into other dimensions.

"Never mind."

"You're such a mutant," Kyle said.

"Yeah, but he's our very own mutant," Patrick said. "All the other kids are jealous."

I reached across the table and flipped open Patrick's assignment book. There was nothing on the page except some doodles. "No homework?" I asked.

"Are you kidding?" Patrick said. "It's the first day."

I glanced down and noticed Mitch's schedule. Most of the classes had *T.P.* next to them. "What's *T.P.?*" I asked.

"Toilet paper," Kyle said. "If you don't know that, you'd better run home and change your underwear."

"Tech prep," Patrick said. "Isn't that what you have?"

"Nope." So that explained why they weren't in my classes. I was dying to ask if they'd noticed Julia, but I didn't want them to think I was obsessed with her or anything. So I sat and listened while they made fun of their teachers.

Patrick was definitely right about avoiding seniors. On the way out of the cafeteria, this big guy knocked my books from under my arm. He grinned and said, "Oops. Must suck to be a freshman." Then he strutted away.

As I was grabbing my stuff, and earning a couple kicks in the rear from passing kids, Kyle sprinted ahead and knocked the guy's books out from under his arm. "Oops to you, too," Kyle said when the guy spun around. "Must suck to lose teeth."

The guy stared at him for a moment. Kyle stared back. Then the guy snatched his books from the floor and walked off.

"Hey, thanks, but you didn't have to do that," I said.

"No one messes with my friends," Kyle said. He'd broken his nose way back in first grade. It had healed kind of crooked, which made him look tough. Everyone figured he liked to fight. The truth is, he broke it falling off a rocking horse. But that didn't matter. Once you had a reputation, good or bad, it stayed with you.

On the way to my next class, I got relieved of my "spare change" by a guy who could work as a debt collector for the Mob. I was glad Kyle wasn't around to try to help me. He would have gotten killed. Though I'd bet Bobby could have taken the guy.

My little miscommunication with *tesseract* was nothing compared to the language barrier that greeted me in my next class. I'd picked Spanish for my foreign language because I figured it would be easier than French or German. It seemed like a great idea until the period started.

The teacher, Ms. de Gaulle, opened her mouth and made some sounds that sort of resembled a sentence, though none of it contained any meaning. We all looked at one another and shrugged. That didn't seem to bother her. She smiled and repeated the sentence.

Everyone stared at her.

She spoke again. And again. Eventually, we figured out that we were supposed to repeat what she said. That seemed to make her happy. It reminded me of when I was little and I used to dream up magic spells. *Abra-ca-dumbo. Hocus mucus. Presto squisho.*

During the rest of the day, I got lost three more times, yelled at twice, and nearly trampled when I headed up a flight of stairs while everyone else on the planet was racing down. My last class was really far from my locker, which was really far from the parking lot. I almost missed the bus. By the time I left Zenger High, my head was stuffed with a jumble of facts and figures, and my backpack weighed eighty-five pounds. Between my homework and a couple comments I couldn't resist adding, I'd already filled a page in my assignment book. At least it would be a short week, since school had started on a Wednesday. If this had been a Monday, I think I would have just quit right then and joined the army.

"Man, high school is awesome," Mouth said when we got on the bus. He looked like he'd been forced through a meat grinder at least twice. His clothes were rumpled, his backpack had footprints on it, and one of his shoelaces was missing. But he seemed happy.

I tuned him out as he launched into more details about his awesome day.

Scott Hudson's Assignment Book

English—Read "The Lottery." Read chapter one in the textbook and answer the questions on page 19. Learn the first twenty vocabulary words.

Art—Read the article on Van Gogh. Sketch something interesting you find in your room. There's that piece of pizza that fell behind my dresser last month.

Algebra—Read pages 7–14. Do the odd-numbered problems. From what I've seen, they're all pretty odd.

Spanish—I don't have a clue what I'm supposed to do. The teacher wrote the assignment on the board in Spanish. What the heck's a *cuaderno?*

History—Read the first three chapters. Answer the questions at the end. Try to stay awake.

Chemistry—Read pages 3–14. Answer the questions on page 15. Count the atoms in your house. For extra credit, count the atoms in your neighborhood.

{four}

Mom was in the kitchen when I got home from school. I thought she was looking through a photo album, but when I got closer I saw it was wallpaper samples.

"You redecorating?" I asked.

She looked up and said, "Hi, hon. How was school?"

"Fine." The page she'd stopped at had a pattern with little rocking horses on it. "Those things are dangerous," I said.

She flipped the book closed. "Would you like a snack?"

"Maybe in a bit. I got a ton of stuff to do." I headed upstairs to face my homework.

I read the story Mr. Franka had assigned for English. It was really good. And creepy enough to give me hope that English would be fun this year. Then I read the article about Van Gogh, which was also pretty interesting, and also sort of creepy in its own way. The vocabulary list wasn't a problem, since I already knew all but one of the words. I tried to decide what to do next, but none of it looked like much fun, so I read a couple more stories from the book. By then, it was time for dinner. Mom had roasted a chicken, with stuffing, mashed potatoes, and gravy. I figured I could get everything done easily enough after we ate.

"How was school?" Dad asked. He'd just gotten home from work, but had already changed out of his button-down shirt. He runs the service department for Linwood Mercedes over in Allentown. He'd rather work on cars than boss around the guys who do the work, and he'd really rather work on classic American muscle cars than hugely expensive luxury vehicles, but the offer was too good to refuse. Besides, if he saves up enough, he can open his own garage someday and get to do what he really wants.

"School was fine." I grabbed the gravy and swamped my chicken.

Dad looked at Mom. "Did you . . . ?"

Mom shook her head.

"What?" I asked.

"Nothing," they both said. Too loudly, and too quickly.

I figured I should let it drop. But I spotted the newspaper over on the counter by the microwave. I went over, lifted it up, and stared at what lay beneath. Two magazines. I spread them out.

No alien Elvises. No six-legged cows. Something much scarier. The first magazine had a smiling baby on the cover. The other showed a smiling woman who looked like she was smuggling a watermelon under her dress. I spun back to face my parents. "Did Bobby get some girl pregnant?" I wasn't ready to be an uncle. And Bobby sure wasn't ready to be a dad.

Another perfect chorus from my parents. "No!"

"Then who . . . ?" I didn't even need to finish the question. Mom's face broadcast the answer.

"We just found out," Dad said. "Dr. Rudrick wanted your mom to take this medicine for her headache, but he needed to make sure she wasn't pregnant first. As it turned out, she was."

A baby . . .

I staggered back to the table. This was so huge, I couldn't even grasp the full meaning. It was like trying to inhale all the air in a beach ball.

Mom reached out and ruffled my hair. "Now don't you worry. You're still my little boy."

A baby . . .

Images flashed through my mind, like a multimedia video from hell. I saw the whole house filled from floor to ceiling with dirty diapers. And puddles of baby puke. Clouds of scented talcum powder drifted through the scene like horror-movie fog. All to the background music of constant crying.

"Quite a surprise, isn't it?" Dad said.

"Yup."

"We wanted to wait a while before we told you," he said, "but I guess you suspected something was going on."

"So now you know our little secret," Mom said. "We're thinking Sean for a boy, and Emily for a girl." She patted her stomach. "Hard to believe there's a tiny life growing in there."

Hard to believe.

"It's a bit of a surprise for all of us," Dad said.

"But a good surprise," Mom said. "I'm glad you know."

They started to eat. Dad worked his way through three big servings of chicken, with lots of gravy. At six-feet-four, he needs huge quantities of fuel to keep going. Mom nibbled one slice of meat and a teaspoon of stuffing.

I kept watching them, as if I could lock away this scene somehow. Keep things the way they were. And I kept looking at Mom, trying to believe that a life was forming inside of her. It had to be some kind of mistake.

Two minutes later, Mom dropped her fork and dashed off. I heard the bathroom door slam shut. A moment after that, I heard the sound of a slice of meat and a teaspoon of stuffing going the wrong way. And I'd been worried about baby puke.

"Think she's okay?" I asked Dad.

"Yeah. It's morning sickness."

"In the evening?"

Dad shrugged. "Whoever named it screwed up. I'll be back in a second." He headed off to the bathroom.

Mom seemed fine when she and Dad returned, but my appetite was shot. Dad was pretty much finished, too. "Just in time for the sports news," he said after we'd cleared the table. "Join me?"

"Great."

"Do you have any homework?" Mom asked.

"Not a lot. I can finish it after this." I followed Dad into the living room. I kept looking at him. He kept looking at me. But not at the same time. We took turns. And we didn't talk about it. Except for two brief conversations.

"Does Bobby know?"

"Not yet. Guess we'd better tell him."

And later:

"Where's it going to sleep?"

"We're turning the spare room into a nursery."

"What about the slot cars? I thought we were going to put a track in there."

"I guess that'll have to wait."

I had a feeling that wasn't the only unhappy change headed my way. I watched the sports news and part of a movie with Dad, then went up to my room and sprawled out on my bed.

Oh

my

God.

Them having a baby was as outrageous as me becoming a father. Not that there was any danger of that happening right now. Everything was fine the way it was. The way it had always been. Bobby was the older brother. I was the younger brother.

I sat up as that sank in. *Older brother.* I was going to be an older brother. What did that mean?

Protector. Teacher. Hero. Me? I'd barely survived my first day of school.

I was brought back to reality by a light tap on my door. Dad popped his head in and asked, "You okay?"

"I'm fine." It was a harmless lie.

He nodded and left.

Maybe I should have asked him if he was okay. This had to be a huge shock for him. But he would probably have lied, too. That's what guys do. If someone cut my head off, the last words whistling through my throat as my face plunged toward the floor would be, "I'm fine."

I said it again, to see if there was any truth at all in those words. Hard to know. It's just as easy to lie to yourself as it is to lie to other people. Maybe easier.

I'm fine. School will be easy. I'm not worried about anything. I'm happy for Mom. It sure will be wonderful to have a baby around the house.

I got back to work. But my thoughts kept drifting. Babies. Babies. Julia. Babies. Julia. If I could have just one date with her, I'd never want anything again. One date, and I'd be happy. Or if I could even just hang out with her, talking about stories and books. That would be so great.

I tried calling Bobby around nine. He'd had his first girlfriend in seventh grade. And his second. And his third. If anyone could give me a couple tips, it would be him.

There was no answer.

Tips about high school would have been nice, too. Today would have been so much easier if I'd had advice from someone who'd already been there. But Bobby hadn't been able to tell me anything useful. What about me? Years from now, when my little brother or sister was ready to start high school, would I remember anything?

I tried to remember my first day of kindergarten. It was like riffling a deck of cards. Mostly blurs, with a couple of solid images flying past. Middle school was a bit clearer, but even that was fading. Would anything be left of my memories of high school fifteen years from now? It was weird to realize I was going to forget things I hadn't even experienced yet.

I looked down at my textbooks. I wasn't ready to tackle history or chemistry. Or algebra. I needed a break. It's not like it would take that long once I got started.

There was an extra notebook on my desk. I picked it up and stared at the blank page for a while, then wrote the date.

• • •

September 5

Listen, you microscopic intruder. Guys don't keep diaries. No way. At least, not any of the guys I hang out with. So this is NOT a diary. Okay? I hope we're clear on that.

So why am I messing up a perfectly good blank notebook? To give you an idea of what high school is like. And maybe give you some tips.

I need to do this now, while I'm still feeling benevolent. Benevolent . . . How's that for a great word? Which brings me to my first piece of advice: be careful with big words. People don't like show-offs. They don't like baby puke, either. So try to keep your food down. Okay?

Right now, I can sort of cope, because you're not real. After you're born, I'll probably hate you. So it's good that I'm doing this now. Maybe it'll make up for all the rotten things I'll do to you later.

Do babies float?

Just kidding. Ha-ha. Of course you'll float. Everyone knows babies are about 90 percent gas. *Pfffttt.* That's a gas sound, in case you didn't figure it out.

I'm going to keep this short, because I've still got some homework. But I should write down the important stuff while it's fresh in my mind.

Scott Hudson's High School Survival Tips

Keep away from seniors.
Keep away from juniors.

It's probably a good idea to avoid sophomores, too, since most of them seem to want revenge for what happened when they were freshmen.

Don't ever kneel. Especially if there are big kids around.

Never wear a dorky hat. Especially if there are big kids around.

Don't carry your books under your arm in a crowded hall.

Try to avoid the bus, even if it means catching a ride from a stranger with a chain saw.

If you're friends with a girl in kindergarten, try to stay friends with her when you get older because otherwise she might forget she ever knew you, and she might get so drop-dead gorgeous you don't have the guts to remind her that you once shared a pack of peanut-butter crackers.

If you're going to break something, a nose is probably better than an arm, since it heals faster and it makes you look tough.

Enough. I'm fading fast. I must be crazy wasting time on this. I better get back to my homework.

Oh—one more thing. Short stories are harder to write than novels. You heard it here first.

I'll try to write more tomorrow. And it's not like you're going anywhere. Sorry I can't be more garrulous at the moment. While I'm gone, see if you can spot vocabulary word number 20 in this paragraph.

{ five }

a hand bursts up through the grave, the bloodless flesh clawing at the soil as a church bell rings in the distance. Slowly, the undead creature emerges, pulling himself free of ground that housed his endless sleep.

Endless sleep?

I wish. I felt like such a zombie. I'd underestimated how much homework I had. Big-time. I'd stayed up until two-fifteen. When I finally got to sleep, I had at least three nightmares about "The Lottery." In one, I was surrounded by a mob of adults who all had baby heads.

I felt so tired, I could cry.

"Good morning," Mom sang when I stumbled into the kitchen. She'd cooked up a big breakfast—eggs, sausages, toast. The smell of food made me gag. I wondered if morning sickness was catching.

"How about something to eat?" she asked.

"Maybe tomorrow . . ." I staggered out. Damn. High school was going to kill me.

I fell asleep on the bus, which was really a bad move, because when I woke up my backpack was missing. So was one of my sneakers. The thought of losing all my homework jolted me awake. I spotted the backpack on the floor by the last row, and had to wait for everyone to walk past me before I could grab it. Which got me shouted at. Luckily, my sneaker was on the seat. Unluckily, it was stuffed with chewing gum and half a Twinkie.

I spotted Patrick, Mitch, and Kyle by the edge of the parking lot, tossing a toy football. I didn't have the energy to hang out. I snuck around them and went inside, stopping at a trash can to scrape out as much of the gum and Twinkie as I could.

I think I dozed some more in homeroom. But at least I was among other freshmen, so nothing bad happened. When I got to English, I noticed the screen was pulled down over the blackboard. I checked around the room. Everyone looked exhausted. Two kids had their heads down on their desks.

"Are we having a movie?" Kelly asked.

Please, I thought. That would be great. They'd turn out the lights and I could take another nap.

Mr. Franka shook his head, but didn't say anything until everyone was seated.

"We should watch *The Princess Bride,*" Julia said. "It's perfect for English class."

My head snapped in her direction, but I managed to strangle my cry of agreement so it ended up sounding like nothing more than a weird cough. That was one of my favorite movies. Life would be so much easier if she'd just say something incredibly stupid so I could kick the habit of worshiping her.

"My friends," Mr. Franka said, "I have a treat for you."

If it was a mattress and a blanket, I'd be happy.

He held up an old book. "But first, a word of explanation.

{3 3}

One of the most popular series from long ago was *Tom Swift*. The key thing about Tom, for our purposes, was that he never just *said* anything. The writer was always ramping things up. Tom would 'exclaim surprisedly,' or 'shout vigorously.'

"Tom's speech habits became so well known that people started making fun of them. It turned into a word game. Ladies and gentlemen, I give you"—he reached down and yanked the cord at the bottom of the screen, sending it clattering back—"the Tom Swifty."

I started reading the writing on the blackboard, and started waking up a bit.

"I'd like a hot dog," Tom said frankly.

"Stop this horse," Tom said haltingly.

"I don't know the words to this song," Tom said humbly.

"They're building new apartments down the road," Tom said constructively.

"I refuse to read Shakespeare," Tom said unwillingly.

A couple kids just stared and said, "Huh?" But I got it right away. I especially liked the last one, because it wasn't as obvious as the others. You had to make the leap from Shakespeare to William, and from there to Will.

"Explain the first one," Mr. Franka said, pointing to me.

"A hot dog is also called a frank," I said. "So using *frankly* makes it a joke."

He nodded. "Very swift of you. Next one?" He called on another kid.

I zoned in and out during the rest of the class as we continued to discuss short stories. When first period ended, I headed for the gym, which was also amazingly well hidden. Like the cafeteria, I finally found it by following my nose.

"Wake up!" someone shouted, ramming me in the shoulder as I reached the locker-room door.

I spun around and yelled back at Kyle. "Knock it off."

"Man, you look like you're wasted," he said.

"Sleep deprivation," I muttered.

He stared at me. "Sleep what?"

"Never mind." I followed him into the locker room. Or tried to. A class of seniors poured out the door with the force of water bursting through a broken dam. I got flattened against the wall in the rush.

"Okay, ladies," a deep voice roared when I finally got inside. "Let's get moving."

Within ten minutes, I found myself wishing I'd been trampled to death in the hallway.

See Scott run.
Run, Scott, run.
See Scott die.
No such luck . . .

We didn't even warm up. As soon as we got into our gym clothes, Mr. Cravutto herded the class outside and tried his best to kill us with an intense session of jumping jacks, squat thrusts, push-ups, sit-ups, throw-ups, and leg lifts. Then we ran in place. After which, for variety, we ran laps. Followed by sprints.

"This sucks," I gasped when I finished my sprint. As far as I could see, phys ed was all phys and no ed.

"That's 'cause you're out of shape," Kyle said.

"I am not. Nobody is in shape for this." I bent over and tried to catch my breath.

"Okay, another lap," Mr. Cravutto screamed. "Jog backward."

Sheesh. He'd probably make us run up the side of the school if he could figure out how. While I was jogging, I kept my mind off the pain by thinking of things that were worse than gym class. It was a short list. There just weren't that many things capable of producing so much misery.

Eventually, we stopped exercising and played soccer, which was fun. Or would have been if I hadn't already been exercised to death. We ran another lap at the end of the period.

"Kick up some dust, you sissies," Mr. Cravutto yelled. For the record, this seemed to be an impossible request to fulfill when running on cinders three days after a heavy rainfall.

We had to take a shower. It was one of the rules. I got in and out as fast as I could. I figured I'd take a real one when I got home. Thank goodness there were only freshmen in the class. The last thing I'd want was to be naked within striking range of a senior. Especially a senior armed with a damp towel. Towels might look soft and fluffy, but in the hands of an expert they can remove a limb.

Next to me, Kyle dried his hair, then stuffed the damp towel into his locker on top of his gym clothes, where it could start the process of putrification. "I told you that would be great," he said when we headed for the hall.

I didn't answer. I was too busy dodging the mob of big kids

who'd burst through the door. I knew if I got swept up in the stream, I'd vanish inside, never to be seen again. At least, not in one piece. I shuddered to think where the next Twinkie could get jammed.

When I got to art class, I figured I should write down my list while it was still fresh in my mind.

Scott Hudson's Guide to Things That Are Worse Than Gym

1. Drinking a half-gallon of lemonade and then taking a six-hour ride across bumpy roads on a bus with no bathroom.
2. Sitting on a cavalry sword that's been dipped in Tabasco sauce.
3. Getting a big smooch from Aunt Zelda before she cleans her false teeth.
4. Getting a big smooch from Aunt Zelda after she cleans her false teeth.
5. Getting your head stuck in a bucketful of dead worms that's been baking in the sun for a week.

We caught up with Mitch and Patrick at lunch. "You guys have gym yet?" I asked them.

Patrick lifted up his gym bag from the floor. "Next period."

Mitch lifted up an empty hand. "I got out of it."

"Out? How?" That was like hearing he'd won the lottery.

"Bad back." He rotated his shoulder, then flinched.

"Yeah, right," Kyle said.

Mitch grinned. "Got a letter from my doctor."

I'd have loved to get out of gym. But, unlike Mitch, I didn't have an uncle with a medical degree.

"Wish I could get out of English," Patrick said.

Kyle nodded. "You got that right."

"Are you kidding? English is great," I said. "I think it's my favorite class."

They stared at me like I'd just admitted I loved to eat crayons dipped in mayonnaise. "Seriously, it's my best class."

"No way," Kyle said. "We spent the whole period memorizing propositions."

"You mean prepositions?" I asked.

Kyle shrugged. "Something like that."

"Whatever you call it," Patrick said, "we got them rammed down our throats."

"Wow. Rammed down. You must be fed up," I said. "Ticked off. Bummed out. Screwed over."

"Very funny," Patrick said. "Kiss off."

I couldn't imagine Mr. Franka making us do that. "Really, we had a great time." I told them about the Tom Swifties.

"That's sort of cool," Patrick said. "You're lucky. Sounds like you got a good class."

"Yeah, it's great." I thought about how small a part of my year English class was going to be, compared to what was happening at home.

Patrick stared at me for a second, then said, "What's wrong?"

"What do you mean?"

"You look strange," he said. "Like something's going on."

"Everything's fine."

I guess Patrick didn't believe my lie. "Is Bobby in trouble again?" he asked.

I shook my head. "Nothing that simple. My mom's having a baby." Wow. It was weird to hear myself say that.

The news earned some gasps of surprise. I looked around the table. Patrick was the youngest in his family. Just like me. Kyle had a sister who was two years younger. Mitch was the third of four kids, but he was only a year older than his younger brother. "Any advice?"

Nothing but shrugs. Except from Kyle, who said, "Tell your mom to stay out of libraries so she doesn't have another mutant bookworm."

"Thanks. I'll pass that along."

I glanced over at Mitch, but he wasn't interested in birth at the moment. From what I could tell, he'd given all his attention to other aspects of biology. He was staring across the cafeteria at a girl with long brown hair. She looked like a young version of that singer he had the hots for.

"Better stop," Kyle said, "or she'll call the cops on you."

Mitch turned his stare toward Kyle. "Obviously, you know nothing about girls."

"And you do?" Kyle said.

Mitch nodded. "She's been checking me out."

"Then go talk with her," Kyle said.

"I will when I'm ready."

"No, you won't," Kyle said. "You're chicken."

"Watch and learn." Mitch got up and strolled across the cafeteria.

"Oh, my God," Patrick said. "He's going to do it."

Kyle shook his head. "This won't be pretty. She'll shoot him right down." He formed a gun with his hands and made shooting sounds.

I figured he was right. The girl was at least a sophomore. No way she'd be interested in a freshman. Still, I couldn't help rooting for Mitch. If just one of us made it out of the cave, that meant there was hope for everyone. And while I'd chew off my own tongue before admitting it out loud, he was probably the best-looking guy in our group.

We all stared when Mitch started talking to the girl. We stared even harder when he sat down next to her. I felt like I was watching a nature film about the mating dances of adolescent humans. Mitch spoke. The girl nodded and smiled. Then she spoke. Lips moved. Words flowed. They looked very much like two people having a conversation. Or exchanging propositions.

"Let's do some Tom Swifties," I said after I got tired of watching.

"Let's stick forks in our eyes," Kyle said. "That would be even more fun."

That made me think of the perfect one. " 'Let's stick forks in our eyes,' Tom said blindly."

" 'And knives,' Tom said cuttingly."

I nodded at Patrick. "Good one. Hey—how about, ' "Cafeteria food makes me gag," Tom said wretchedly.' "

Patrick and I kept at it until the bell rang.

"You guys are so hopeless," Kyle said as he dashed out.

Right after I left the cafeteria, a scary-looking senior was nice enough to help me get rid of the coins that were jangling in my pocket. He was wearing a plain white T-shirt, tucked into jeans, and had the sort of arm muscles that couldn't possibly have been made out of anything organic. My best guess was either granite or steel.

He made it sound like a voluntary act. "Got any spare change?" But the look in his eyes told me there was only one safe answer. The last time I'd seen eyes that deadly, I'd been at the hyena cage at the zoo. I handed over my change. It was better than handing over my teeth. I was happy I'd had a chance to eat first.

He actually said, "Thanks." Like I was doing him a favor. Later, I heard a couple other freshmen talking about the guy. His name was Wesley Cobble, and nearly everyone in the school was afraid of him.

Somehow, I managed to stay awake through the rest of the day. Not that it made any difference in Spanish. Things were just as confusing as they'd been yesterday. "'Spanish makes no sense,' Scott said unknowingly." Unwittingly. Incomprehensibly.

In history, while I was pretending to take notes, I jotted down some more Tom Swifties. A couple were so funny, I had to bite the inside of my cheek to keep from laughing.

Much to my amazement, I made it through the day.

I sat behind Sheldon on the ride home. It worked. The big kids smacked him and left me alone. If I could figure out some way to make life-size Sheldon Murmbower decoys, I'd be rich. Every freshman on the planet would buy one.

The minute I got home, I headed for the shower. I cranked

the faucets up full blast. It felt great. For about sixty seconds. Then the hot water ran out. I ran out, too.

"Mom," I shouted, "there's no hot water."

"Sorry," she yelled back. "I'm washing the new sheets I bought for the baby."

I toweled off, grabbed my robe, and worked on my homework until the wash was done, then stepped back in the shower.

The phone rang as soon as I got out.

"Want to go bowling?" Kyle asked.

"It's a school night," I said.

"So?"

"So I have homework."

"So do it later."

"I can't. I've got plans for later."

"Like what?"

"Like sleep."

"You're no fun anymore."

"Thanks."

"Not that you were all that much fun before, either."

"Thanks again."

"We'll be at Devon Lanes if you change your mind."

As soon as I hung up, I regretted saying I couldn't go. A couple games wouldn't take all that long. But if I showed up now, Kyle would give me a hard time about mentioning my homework. I decided I'd better just get it over with. So once again, I sat at my desk, face-to-face with a wad of assignments, and instantly looked around the room for some way to avoid starting my work.

• • •

September 6

Hey—stomach virus—I have a question for you. What's the point in giving clean sheets to someone who's going to spurt all sorts of fluids from every body cavity? Give up? Yeah; me, too. It would make more sense to get you a wading pool than a crib. At least then we could hose it off when it got too yucky. Look up *viscous* when you get a chance. If you thought I said *vicious,* you need to pay more attention. *Vicious* is how you make me feel. *Viscous* describes the stuff that flows from you.

You're driving Mom crazy, you realize. But you probably don't care since you'll have clean sheets. And I'll have cold showers.

But I'm not so coldhearted that I don't want to share what I've learned. So here's a tip. Start planning now for a way to get out of gym. It's never too early to work on your excuses. And here's today's survival rule: don't carry loose coins in your pants. The sound attracts thugs who'll tap your pocket and say, "Gimme some change." At which point, you either "give 'em some change" or get hurt.

My day wasn't all disaster. We did something totally cool in English. It's called *Tom Swifties.* I wrote a couple pretty good ones. Here—check these out.

Scott Hudson's Tom Swifties

"Who turned off the lights?" Tom said dimly.

"I lost my legs right below the ankles," Tom said defeatedly.

"I lost my fingers," Tom said disjointedly.

"I lost my wrists," Tom said offhandedly.

"I lost my elbows," Tom said disarmingly.

"I lost my ribs," Tom said decidedly.

"The worms are eating my organs," Tom said wholeheartedly.

"I've been sliced in half," Tom said intuitively.

Well, that's my list. Did you get the last one? If not, think about how *in half* means *in two.*

Okay. Enough for now. "Time to do my homework," Scott said slavishly. "I can't wait for Saturday," Scott said weakly. "Okay, I'll stop now," Scott said. Endlessly.

You know what? These aren't bad. I wonder whether Julia would think they're funny. Hard to tell. Guys and girls don't always have the same sense of humor. But that's something I'll let you find out for yourself. You quivering sack of viscous fluids.

{ six }

I managed to get a bit more sleep Thursday night, but still nowhere near enough. I realized I was going to be a zombie for the next four years.

"You look tired," Mom said when I went down to breakfast.

I nodded. "A bit." I noticed she looked tired, too.

She slid a plate of fresh-baked blueberry muffins in front of me. "Well, don't work too hard."

As I reached for a muffin, she added, "But work hard enough. Okay?"

"I will. You don't have to worry." I broke the muffin in half and watched the rising steam.

"I guess, the way you like to read, you'll have an easier time in school than Bobby did."

"Yeah. It helps if you like books." I ate the muffin, then grabbed another to eat on the way to the bus. This time, I made sure not to fall asleep during the ride.

My exhaustion might help explain my act of stupidity. When I got to English class, I pulled out my list of Tom Swifties and passed them to Kelly. That was step number one in my master plan. I figured she'd laugh, then Julia would ask her what was so funny, and Kelly would pass them over.

The first part worked. Kelly laughed. I could tell when she got near the end because she blurted out that *ewwwww* sound girls make when they bump into something especially gross. It was probably *wholeheartedly* that pushed her over the edge. I took it as an *ewwww* of appreciation, since she still laughed. Vicky Estridge leaned over from the seat behind Kelly and asked, "What's so funny?" Kelly passed the list to her. After an *eww* or two, Vicky gave it to the kid on her right. Before I could get the list back, Mr. Franka came in and hit us with a quiz.

By the end of the period, I didn't have a clue about what happened to the paper, or whether Julia even saw it. "I lost my Tom Swifties," Scott said listlessly.

I was almost too tired to care. At least it was Friday. I had the whole weekend ahead of me to sleep. Or to waste time sharing my thoughts with imaginary creatures.

September 7

So, you formless clump of cells, you're probably wondering whether I learned anything today. You bet.

Listen carefully. This is important. Never try to impress anyone. Especially not a girl. It won't work. You'll just end up feeling stupid. (If you're a girl yourself, just ignore this. But since I don't have a clue about how to talk to girls, and couldn't possibly have any advice for one, I'm going to assume you're a guy.)

Meanwhile, the workload keeps on growing. We're

starting a novel in English. *To Kill a Mockingbird.* Weird title. I wonder if there's a sequel where they make fun of hawks. You know, *To Mock a Killing Bird.* Sorry. That was really awful. I must be more tired than I realized.

But that's not going to stop me from going to the movies. I'd ask you to come, but I don't think the seats are fluid-proof, you wet, oozing mess of ichor.

I met up with Kyle and Patrick in front of the Cinema Twelve on Milford Street. "Where's Mitch?" I asked after I bought my ticket.

"Don't know," Patrick said. "He's out somewhere, I guess."

"Screw him," Kyle said. "I'm not missing the previews." He headed through the doors.

Patrick and I followed him. *This will work,* I thought as I dropped down in my seat. I could get my homework done and still have a normal social life. I figured I'd catch up on my sleep, then tackle the homework on Saturday afternoon. There was nothing I liked more than sleeping late on the weekend.

It was a perfect plan, except that the phone woke me the next morning. I figured someone would get it, but it rang four times. Then I heard the answering machine from the living room downstairs.

Still half asleep, I listened to Bobby's voice. "Someone pick up. Come on. Please?"

I thought about crawling out of bed, but I knew I had a shot at falling back to sleep if I stayed where I was.

"Anyone there?"

He sounded desperate. But I was desperate for sleep.

"I only get one phone call."

One phone call? Shoot. I knew what that meant. I went downstairs and picked up the phone. "It's me," I said.

"Is Mom there?"

"Yeah." I could hear the sound of the dryer. "I think she's in the basement. What'd you do?"

"Nothing. Just get Mom."

"Hang on." I went down to the basement. When I told Mom that Bobby was on the phone, she raced up the stairs. Her smile didn't last long. It was pretty easy to figure most of it out from listening to her half of the conversation.

"The police station? Oh Bobby, what did you . . . So it was just parking tickets? How many? Oh, my. That's a lot. If you didn't have the money, you should have told us. No, it doesn't matter if you don't have the car anymore. You still have to pay the tickets. Don't worry. We'll get it all straightened out. No, I can't do that. I have to tell him. We'll be there right away. I love you. Bye."

She sighed, hung up, and went to get Dad.

"He's in jail?" I asked when they came downstairs.

"It's nothing," Mom said. "Just a little misunderstanding."

They headed out. I headed upstairs. I was too wound up to go back to sleep. So I picked up the notebook.

September 8
Bobby's in trouble. It's no big deal. He's had a lot of bad luck recently. He totaled his car last month. He wasn't hurt. Nobody else was, either. Just the tree.

I wonder what it felt like for you when Mom ran up the stairs. Fun ride? Want me to see if I can get her on a roller coaster?

The movie was awful, by the way. I'm still glad I went out. I think Kyle's pissed at Mitch because Mitch found a girlfriend. Patrick doesn't seem to care. I'm not sure how I feel about it. No, that's a lie. I wish it was me.

Oh crap, this is starting to sound like a diary. Next thing I know, I'll be telling you who my dream date is. Oh crap again. I already did that, didn't I?

"Guess who's home?" Mom called from downstairs.

I closed my algebra book. Two o'clock already. I'd started around noon. Wow. Homework could really swallow time. Someday, I expect to look up from a textbook and discover that I'm fifty.

I ran into Bobby halfway down the steps. He had a pile of clothes in his arms—mostly flannel shirts and jeans, topped with T-shirts, socks, and stuff. As high as they were stacked, he could still see over them.

"Hey, squirt, give us a hand." He nodded in the direction of the front door.

"Sure." I squeezed past him and went out to the driveway, where Dad had left the car. The trunk was filled with Bobby's stuff. Dad took Bobby's tool kit into the garage.

"He's staying here for a while," Mom said, passing me a box of CDs. I noticed Bobby's Fender Stratocaster guitar in the backseat.

I helped bring in the rest of his stuff, then sat in his room while he hung up his clothes.

"You move out of your place?" I asked.

He shrugged. "Sort of. I owed rent."

"How come?"

"No money."

"What about your job?"

"I was late a bunch. I had to walk 'cause of the car getting totaled. They got an attitude about it and fired me. I was looking for another job. But it's tough without wheels."

"Yeah. Must be." I flipped through his movie collection. He had some pretty good action films. "You remember being a freshman?"

He shook his head. "I'm not even sure I remember last night. Why?"

"Nothing . . ."

"What is it? A girl?"

"How'd you know?"

He threw a shirt at my head. "It's always a girl. So what's the problem?"

"Well, how'd you get girls to notice you?"

"I never thought about it. I guess they just notice me. They'll notice you, too. You're a Hudson. We've got the power." He flashed me a grin.

Right. They'll notice me. If I paint myself orange and glue hamsters to my shirt.

I helped him put his movies and music on his shelves. I was dying to find out how he felt about the baby. Mom and Dad

{50}

must have told him by now. But I wasn't sure he'd even want to talk about that.

When I got up to leave, Bobby said, "It's all going to change, you know."

"What? School?"

He shook his head and pointed downstairs. "Everything. After the baby's born, they won't have time for anything else."

"Sure they will."

Bobby stared at me. "Stop lying to yourself. I was only four when you were born, but I can remember how much it changed things."

"I'm not lying to myself," I said. It was a lie I really wanted to believe. "Nothing's going to change."

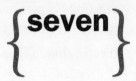

{ **seven** }

monday morning, I plunged myself into my first full week of school. It didn't start out much different from my first three days. Mouth talked nonstop from the moment he caught sight of me. Julia didn't even glance in my direction. I glanced in hers. She seemed to grow more gorgeous each day. At this rate, I figured I'd explode sometime around mid-November. I'd look at her and just blow apart in a gruesome hydraulic disaster.

At least the Sheldon shield worked. I had a feeling that by the time he graduates, the accumulated smacks will have turned his brain into some sort of liquid resembling bean soup.

Maybe Julia didn't notice me, but someone else did. All through English, Mr. Franka kept looking at me with this amused smile. I honestly didn't have a clue what was going on. I even checked under my nose a couple times, to make sure nothing was dangling.

"Scott," he said to me at the end of class, "I need to ask you something." He held up a piece of paper. When I recognized it, I thought about making a dash for the door. But I figured he was fast enough to run me down.

I also figured he was going to give me a lecture because of all the things I wrote about losing legs and arms and stuff. I was really really really glad I didn't put down the ones that I thought of later, like "Clean the toilet seat," said Tom peevishly. Or "Who sneezed on my hamburger," said Tom snottily.

Mr. Franka caught me by surprise. "You're very creative, Scott. Have you thought about joining the school paper?"

I expressed my great creativity by saying, "Huh?"

"They could use you on staff. What do you think?"

"No thanks." I couldn't believe I wasn't in trouble. But I didn't want to join the paper. I already had too much to do.

"There's a perfect opening for you," Mr. Franka said.

"What?"

"Book reviews. With your wit, I suspect you'd be good."

Book reviews? When he mentioned that, these fantasies flashed through my mind. It was like someone pointed out a road I'd never noticed. I could see myself doing it.

Yeah, right. In my spare time.

"Look. Thanks. It's cool you offered, but I'm pretty busy. You wouldn't believe how much work they load you down with in honors English. The teacher is brutal."

To my relief, he grinned. "Yeah, I've heard that guy's a jerk. No problem. Maybe next year."

The rest of the day, I found myself making up book reviews in my head. But as I walked toward my front door, the weight of my backpack dragged me down into the real world.

Not that the real world didn't have rewards. The moment I stepped inside, I sniffed magic. Mom had been baking. Fresh cherry pie is the perfect after-school snack. Add vanilla ice cream and it goes beyond perfection. Heat. Cold. Sweet. Sour. Heaven.

I vacuumed the first piece. I paced myself on the second, talking with Mom while I ate. She was over by the counter, trimming chicken breasts.

"Did anyone in our family ever go to college?" I asked.

Mom frowned, as if trying to identify a stranger in a photograph, then said, "Not that I know of. Your aunt Doreen went to business school for a year. That's sort of like college."

"What about on Dad's side?"

"His people have always been good with their hands." She trimmed another piece of chicken, then said, "Why?"

"No reason. Just wondering."

Mom smiled at me. "There's a first time for everything."

The rest of the school week zipped past pretty quickly. After losing two more hats, Mouth switched to a jacket with a hood. Another mistake. Wednesday, I saw a couple seniors hang him from the top of a door by the wood shop. He finally managed to get free when he slipped out of the sleeves.

I saw Kyle with some seniors the next day. One of them pushed him. I figured there'd be a fight. But they all started laughing and pushing one another. I guess he knew them from somewhere.

Mitch ate lunch with his girlfriend now, instead of with us. I didn't blame him. Outside the cafeteria, I never even saw him in school. I guess we just traveled different paths.

For the most part, high school had become a matter of life and death. Mr. Cravutto tried his best to kill us with exercise. Ms. Flutemeyer tried to slay us with quadratic equations. Mr. Ferragamo bored us to death with names and dates from the musty past. Ms. Balmer drowned us in chemical formulas.

On the other hand, Mr. Franka taught us all sorts of cool stuff. And on the third hand, Spanish class was still a total mystery.

September 14

Hey, you fluid-dwelling piece of protoplasm. You might notice that it's been nearly a week since I've written anything here. I've been too busy. But since you aren't even born yet, I guess that's not a problem. Time doesn't exist for you. At least I hope not. If it does, you're probably bored out of your skull. If you even have a skull, yet. Or a brain.

Yuck. I wonder if your head is all squishy. To tell the truth, I know hardly anything about fetuses. And I plan to keep it that way. Though I saw one with two heads last year when Bobby took me to a carnival. I think it was fake. Speaking of which, don't ever pay money to see "the world's largest rat." It's actually a capybara. They're supposed to be that size.

I'd bet anything you were too lazy to go get a dictionary when I mentioned *ichor*. Too bad. I'm not telling you what it means.

Hey—you'll like this. We read "The Gift of the Magi" in

English. It's one of the most famous stories ever. It's really short, so we read it right in class. I spotted something weird at the beginning. There's a mistake. I pointed it out to Mr. Franka. He said he'd never noticed. Here. I'll write down the opening, to see if you can spot the problem.

One dollar and eighty-seven cents. That was all. And sixty cents of it was in pennies. Pennies saved one and two at a time by bulldozing the grocer and the vegetable man and the butcher until one's cheeks burned with the silent imputation of parsimony that such close dealing implied. Three times Della counted it. One dollar and eighty-seven cents. And the next day would be Christmas.

Find anything? I'll let you think about it for a couple days. I'll read the whole story to you sometime. It's pretty awesome. Here's a confession—I had to look up *imputation* and *parsimony*.

I'm outta here. I'm not going to blow Friday night sitting in my room writing notes to a cluster of goo.

"What's the plan?" I asked when I got to Kyle's house.

"Football game?" Patrick suggested.

"That wouldn't be much fun," I said. I liked pro ball and pickup games, but the last thing I wanted was to drag myself back to the school right now.

"Shows what you know," Kyle said. "It's got nothing to do with football. Everyone goes. It's a chance to hang out."

"It's a chance to let the seniors get their hands on us," I said. "After they're all worked up from watching two or three hours of violence." I wondered whether Wesley Cobble went to the games. He didn't seem like the school-spirit sort, but he might appreciate the convenience of having so many victims packed together in one place.

"Don't be such a wuss." Kyle turned to Patrick. "Is it at home?"

Patrick shook his head. "It's at Hershorn."

"We could go to Mitch's," I said. "We haven't raced cars in a while." Mitch had an awesome slot-car track in his basement.

"Mitch isn't around," Kyle said. "He's hanging out with that girl."

"Are you serious?" I asked. "They aren't dating, are they?"

Kyle sneered. "Yup. For now. They won't last a week. You'll see. She'll dump him fast."

I looked over at Patrick. "Any ideas?"

"Rent a video?"

That's what we ended up doing. In the movie, the dorky high school kid ended up with the hot girl. Obviously, it was a fantasy.

When I got home, I found Dad in the kitchen with a bucket of wings. "Want to help?" he asked.

"Sure." I grabbed the milk from the fridge and joined him. We had our work cut out for us. The bucket was nearly full.

"So how's school going?" Dad asked.

"Good."

"Glad to hear it." He slid the bucket toward me.

"Dad?"

"Yeah?"

"Did Mom notice you right away?"

He shook his head. "Nope."

"So what did you do?"

"Showed up."

"Where?"

"Wherever."

"So you showed up wherever she was?"

"Or wherever she might be."

"That must have taken a lot of time," I said.

Dad shrugged. "Worth it."

We finished the bucket, and I slept far into Saturday afternoon.

September 15

You have no idea what you're doing to Mom. She keeps getting cravings. Like she'll suddenly decide she wants fried shrimp. So Dad runs out to Long John Silver's. When he gets home, Mom takes one bite and that's it. Craving satisfied. Which leaves a ton of shrimp. There's no way you can let fried shrimp go to waste. So Dad and I eat them. The next day, Mom wants chocolate ice cream. Dad buys her a quart. She eats a spoonful or two. The rest is ours. Last night, it was wings.

Dad's starting to put on a few pounds. I'd probably be

bloating up, too, if I wasn't burning ten zillion calories in gym class.

I've yet to see anything good about being pregnant.

Sunday, after lunch, I was in my room reading the last chapter of *To Kill a Mockingbird*. It was so good, I hated to close the book and admit that it was finished. I wanted to spend more time with Scout and Dill and Atticus Finch.

A minute or two after I reached the last line, I heard Bobby come out of his room.

"Hey," I said, catching him in the hall. I held out the book. "Perfect timing. This is really good. I don't have to turn it in for a couple days. Want to read it?" I figured he had plenty of free time, since he hadn't found a job yet.

He stared at my hand as if I'd offered him a slab of month-old uncooked pork.

"It's really good. Honest. There's this girl named Scout. She's just a little kid, but she's really cool. And she has a brother who—"

"Not now," Bobby said. "Give me a break. I'm not even awake yet. I was out real late. Okay?"

"Yeah. Okay."

As I started to walk off, he said, "Hey, if the folks let me borrow a car, we can do something later. Want to?"

"Sure."

I went downstairs. I could hear Dad out in the garage. Mom was in the kitchen, making applesauce. "This is pretty good," I said, holding up the book. "You want to read it?"

She looked at the cover and smiled. "That is a good one."

"You read it already?" I asked.

"I saw it. What a wonderful movie."

"So maybe you'd like the book."

"Hard to imagine it could be as good as the movie. Besides, I've got plenty to read." She pointed over to the kitchen table at a stack of baby magazines, then dipped a spoon in the sauce and held it out to me. "Taste?"

"Absolutely."

"Need more cinnamon?"

"Nope. It's perfect. You sure you wouldn't like to read something different for a change?"

"Why don't you read some of it to me while I cook? How would that be?"

"Great." I sat down and opened the book, and started to read. It felt strange. Not counting school, I'd never read to anyone before. It was also sort of nice. Right after I finished chapter three, Bobby came down.

"Can I borrow the car?" he asked.

"Sure," Mom said. "Just be careful."

"I will." Bobby turned toward me. "Coming?"

I looked over at Mom. "Go ahead," she said. "I've got a million things to do. But thanks, I enjoyed that."

Bobby grabbed the spare keys from the hook by the door and we headed out.

"So what do you want to do?" Bobby asked.

There was a great used-book store just outside of town, but I didn't think Bobby would go for that. He liked to hang out at the music stores, but since I didn't play an instrument—not counting one disastrous month spent wrestling with a trombone in sixth grade—all I could do was look at the guitars and pretend I was a rock star for about ten minutes, until reality stomped down on my imagination.

"How about slot cars?" I said. "We could go to Hobby-Land." That was pretty far away, but it was the nearest place with a track.

"Sure," Bobby said. "Anytime I can go way too fast without hurting anybody, I'm good." As he pulled out of the driveway, he said, "Hey, doesn't Mitch have a setup?"

"I haven't seen him in a while. He's been kind of busy."

"Yeah. School will do that to you if you aren't careful."

I didn't say much more until we'd pulled into the parking lot at HobbyLand. Finally, I told Bobby, "Mitch's got a girlfriend."

"Way to go, Mitch!" Bobby said.

I guess my silence spoke for me, because Bobby glanced over and said, "Oops. You don't have one?"

"Not yet. I got my eye on someone," I said, trying to sound like success was within reach.

"Good deal."

We only got to race for about fifteen minutes. Then the owner kicked us out because Bobby kept driving too fast and flying off the track. So we went to the music store.

September 16

I finished *To Kill a Mockingbird.* It's awesome. I'd bet Dad would like it because the father in the book is so cool. He's quiet, but he's not a wimp. He kind of reminds me of Dad.

We're starting a new book in English pretty soon. How's this for weird—I'll be reading *The Outsiders.* And you, my unborn, unformed, uninvited sibling, are the ultimate insider. Ewww.

Sibling. Cool word. But you need a name. I know it's going to be Sean or Emily, but Sean-or-Emily is kind of awkward. And kind of weird. Unless you're hoping to work in a carnival. Maybe I can combine them. Seanily? Emean? Semily? Wait, I've got it. Smelly. There you go. It's perfect. It fits you in so many ways. Fits like a glove. Or a bulging diaper.

Oh. Did you figure out the problem with "The Gift of the Magi"? She had $1.87, and 60 cents of that was in pennies. But what does that leave? It leaves $1.27. So she must have had more pennies. I can't see any way to get $1.27 without them. Unless they had two-cent pieces back then.

Bye, Smelly. Talk to you later.

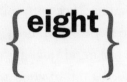
{ **eight** }

there's really only one thing that separates people from dogs. Our ears don't twitch forward when we hear something exciting. Thank goodness. Otherwise, I'd have spilled my secret to the world Tuesday morning in English class.

Up front, Mr. Franka was telling us about similes, metaphors, and other descriptive language. To my right, Kelly was whispering to Julia in a voice as hushed as the rustle of a single-ply tissue. Oh crap, I suck at similes. Anyhow, Kelly was talking. Quietly.

"Did you finish your article for the paper?" she asked.

That was the point when my ears would have pitched forward like a dog who hears his master opening a can of extra-chunky beef stew with an electric can opener.

Julia nodded, sending the shaggy ends of her hair dancing like kids in a mosh pit. I didn't know she was on the paper.

I found it hard to concentrate during the rest of the class. My mind ran elsewhere, like a train that had slipped off the rails. No, that wasn't right. A derailed train usually doesn't get very far. Anyhow, time crawled along like a sleepwalking snail dragging a history book.

After class, I rushed up to see Mr. Franka. "I've been think-ing about what you said. It would be fun to write book re-views." I was running titles through my mind, picking out which book I wanted to do first. I'd read a ton of good stuff over the summer.

"I'm sorry, Scott," he said. "Since you weren't interested, I found someone else."

"Oh." I could feel myself droop like a cheap basketball that was left out on the lawn all winter.

"But you can still join the staff. Just show up tomorrow af-ter school for the meeting. I'm sure they can make good use of your talents."

"Great. I'll be there." I figured there were other cool things I could cover, like movies or something. Whatever I ended up writing, at least I'd get to spend some time in a small group with Julia.

I wondered whether she remembered that we were in kindergarten together. We'd shared an easel once. I was on one side, painting a pirate. She was on the other side. I don't know what she was painting. Probably not a pirate.

I had a hard time finding the meeting room the next day, so I was the last one there. When I walked in, I saw a girl wearing a tight green top and a long denim skirt. The top was made out of that thin, stretchy material.

"Hi, Scott," she said. "I'm Mandy. I heard you might be joining us. That's great. We could really use you." She smiled at me like she meant it. I think it was the first time a senior had looked at me as anything other than a piggy bank, punching bag, or doormat. Especially a cute senior with reddish blond hair and freckles. Did I mention the top?

"It sounds like fun." I glanced at the dozen or so kids who sat around the table. Julia was there, looking even more beautiful than Mandy. Mouth was explaining something to her about his appendix. Apparently, he had it in a jar at home. Or maybe he had pieces of it in two different jars. That part wasn't really clear. I could see Julia's eyes starting to glaze. I tried to stop listening, but it was sort of like watching an accident.

"So I guess you'll be doing football," Mandy said.

I pulled my eyes away from Mouth and Julia. But not my brain. Again, I managed to leap to new creative heights. "What?"

Mandy pointed at my shirt. "None of us is much of a sports fan. We're into food, movies, and music, and stuff like that. But we've got to cover sports. So we're glad you're here."

I'd forgotten I was wearing my Baltimore Ravens T-shirt. Mom bought it for me because I liked Edgar Allan Poe. The Ravens were named after that poem of his.

As I tried to think of some way to explain that I wasn't interested in covering sports, Mandy leafed through a folder in front of her, then handed me a sheet of paper. "Here's the schedule. The games are all on Friday." She smiled, then pointed to an empty chair. "Have a seat."

Between the smile and the top, I would have sat in a bucket of sulfuric acid if she'd asked me. Once my butt hit the chair, the reality hit home. *Sports? Friday?* That was my night out. Could it get any worse?

Mandy turned to Mouth. "How's your first book review coming?"

"It's coming along great." He pulled a mangled sheet of notebook paper from his backpack. "Want to hear what I have so far?"

Mandy shook her head. "I'd rather wait until it's done." She softened the blow with a smile. Though I was pretty sure it wasn't as nice as the one she'd given me.

Mouth? Book reviews? I was afraid to discover what my next surprise would be.

The suspense didn't last long. A couple of minutes later, Mandy said to Julia, "Thanks for writing this week's guest column."

Guest column? Equations flashed through my mind. Guest = just visiting = not here each week = Scott's screwed.

"It was fun," Julia said. "Do you want me to stick around for the rest of the meeting?"

Mandy shook her head. "No need. You can go."

Julia smiled that heart-melting smile of hers and left the room.

When the meeting let out, I called home to see if I could get a ride from Mom.

"She's out," Bobby said. "Went to look for curtains for the nursery."

"There are already curtains in there," I said.

"I know."

"So why do we need new ones?"

"Beats me. Hey, I'd pick you up if I had a car."

"Yeah. I know. Thanks."

So, to make the day even more special, I had to hike into town to catch a metro bus. But I didn't have to go by myself. Mouth joined me. As luck would have it, he was still eager to share the details of his appendix operation.

September 19

Hey, Smelly. Major advice—be careful what you wear. I realize this will be out of your control for a while, but you should start picking your own clothes as soon as possible.

Speaking of which, the bad news is that Mom loves Winnie-the-Pooh. So you're going to be wearing tons of that stuff. Have you ever noticed that Piglet looks like some sort of larval grub with ears? And, if you ask me, Tigger belongs in rehab. But there's something even worse. The Poohster himself. You might as well get used to having people point at you and say, "There's Pooh on your shirt."

That's your problem. My problem is I'm the school paper's sports reporter. The *Zenger Gazette* isn't monthly. I'm going to be writing an article every single week.

And here's another warning. Assuming you're a guy, you're going to do some extremely crazy things just for the chance of getting close to a girl who's caught your attention. I could stand behind you all day and scream "DON'T DO IT!" at the top of my lungs. Wouldn't matter. It's the way we're wired.

You see, guys have certain basic needs. Food, shelter, clothing, girlfriends. Guess which one isn't provided by our parents or the local government? So, for reasons totally beyond my control, I'm Mandy's sports slave. Look up the word *Pavlovian* when you have a chance. I guess you could also look up *nincompoop*. Might as well add *fartbrain* to the list, though I imagine it's not in the dictionary. It would make a great title if I ever write an autobiography. *My Life as a Fartbrain.*

And if you turn out to be a girl, all I can say is take pity on us guys. Okay? But, as I said, I'm just going to assume you're a guy.

I've learned my lesson. I'm never, ever going to try to get Julia to notice me again.

Oh—one final thing. Mom thinks there are butterflies on your new curtains. But I happen to know they're a rare form of vampire moth. Sleep tight. Sweet dreams. Don't let the dead bugs bite.

{ **nine** }

greetings, sports fans. This is Scott Hudson, reporting live from the morning bus ride. Even at this early hour, I see a variety of events taking place.

A hearty game of Smack the Sheldon was going on right in front of me. I could just imagine judges holding up scorecards after each round. In the back, kids were aisle surfing, trying to stand and keep their balance while our driver swung around corners on two wheels and yelled at them to sit. Out the window, on the roads all around us, there was a combination auto race/demolition-derby going on.

Kyle and Patrick were chucking a football in the parking lot when we got to school.

"I'm open," I shouted.

Patrick tossed me the ball. I jogged toward them and flipped a lateral to Kyle.

"Looks like I'm going to the game tomorrow," I said.

"Change your mind?" Patrick asked.

"No choice. I'm covering it for the paper."

"Get out of here."

"Really. I am."

"You serious?"

"Yup."

Patrick grinned. "Pretty cool."

Hey, maybe it was cool. I hadn't said it out loud until now. But I sort of liked the sound of it. *I'm covering it for the paper.* Scott Hudson, sports reporter.

Bonk!

The ball bounced off my head.

"Nice catch," Kyle said.

I picked up the ball, faked high, and nailed him in the gut. Not as satisfying as a head shot, but it would do.

The bell rang, robbing Kyle of an opportunity to retaliate.

The rest of the day passed without any major triumphs or disasters. Though Spanish grew even more perplexing. We'd been repeating sentences for two whole weeks. Today, Ms. de Gaulle passed out textbooks. They were all in Spanish. Nothing inside resembled anything we'd been doing. I glanced around the room. It was obvious that everyone else was just as lost.

When I got home, I found Bobby in his room, playing his guitar. "Guess what? I'm on the school paper."

"Why'd you want to do that? The paper's for geeks."

"No way. You should see the editor. She's hot."

"What's her name?"

"Mandy."

"Oh yeah." Bobby nodded. "I remember her. She wears these killer tops. I think we went out once, the year before last. She's on the paper?"

"Yup."

He patted me on the shoulder. "Way to go, little brother. You can take up where I left off."

Before I could even think of a response, I heard a big-time rumbling sound from outside and felt the floor vibrate.

Bobby's eyes opened wide. "Corvette," he said.

"No way." I refused to believe that anyone could identify a car just from the sound. Not even Bobby, who had a great ear.

"Sixty-three," he added.

"Not a chance."

"Bet you five dollars."

"You're on."

We raced to his window. A Corvette was blowing oily smoke out the tailpipe as it crawled along the driveway.

"I wonder whose it is," I said.

"Let's find out."

Bobby and I ran downstairs. The car wasn't in the driveway. It was in the garage.

"Traded the Taurus," Dad said when Mom, Bobby, and I joined him. "Got a deal on it. With a bit of work, she'll be a gem."

I can't say for sure, but I think he looked at that Corvette the same way I looked at Julia. The main difference being Julia wasn't going to come live in our garage. Or make the walls vibrate.

"Sweet," Bobby said. "Sixty-three?"

Dad nodded. I sighed and dug out my wallet.

Mom snorted, shook her head, and walked back inside

without saying a word. Dad and Bobby popped the hood and started discussing what to do first. Terms like *compression, camshaft,* and *valve covers* drifted through the air.

"Want to help?" Dad asked.

"Maybe later. I have homework." It was a really cool car on the outside. But once the hood was lifted, I was lost. Looking at the engine was like looking at a page of Spanish.

Back inside, Mom was muttering something about men and their stupid toys. "If he goes near my Subaru, I'll shoot him," she said.

I glanced toward the garage. "Are you *sure* I'm not adopted?"

Mom smiled and put a hand on my shoulder. "Hon, I was there when you were born."

"Maybe I got switched."

She shook her head. "Your aunt Jill followed you all the way down to the nursery just to make sure nobody made any mistakes." She put both hands on my shoulders and stared at my face for a moment. "You got your dad's eyes and my dad's chin. There's no escaping it. You're a Hudson."

"But I'm so bad with tools."

"That's not what makes you who you are. You, Bobby, and your dad—as different as you are—you've got good hearts. That's what matters."

I brought my homework to the kitchen, pulled up a stool by the counter, and hung out with Mom while she made a pie crust. I didn't know if I had a good heart, but by the time she was done, I definitely had a good and hearty appetite.

• • •

"I'm going to the football game," I told the folks right after dinner.

"Have fun," Mom said. "Wear a scarf. It's chilly."

"Want a ride?" Dad asked, giving me a little head shake that erased the scarf command. "I think the 'vette can make it that far."

"That would be cool. Thanks. But Patrick's picking me up."

After Patrick's dad dropped us off, we met Kyle in the bleachers. I checked to see who else was there. No sign of Wesley Cobble, which meant I'd probably make it to halftime with the snack money I'd brought.

As the teams lined up for the kickoff, I pulled out a notebook and got ready to describe the highlights. Within five minutes, we were behind by two touchdowns. At the end of the first quarter, the other team brought in their second-string players. By the end of the half, we were behind 31 to 0.

"We weren't that bad last year, were we?" I asked Patrick.

He shook his head. "All the good players graduated. This is pretty sad."

"Let's get out of here," Kyle said.

"I can't."

"Maybe you can't," he said. "But we can."

"You mind if we split?" Patrick asked.

"Go ahead," I told him. "I don't blame you. I wouldn't stay if I didn't have to."

He called his dad. Then he and Kyle took off. Which sucked. I'd have stayed if they'd been stuck here.

The second half was just as painful as the first. When the

game ended, I walked home. It was about two and a half miles, but it was a nice break after sitting there for so long. And it was a nice way to delay getting to work. I guess I was supposed to write some sort of rah-rah article. What could I say? Only one thing came to mind. I wrote it down when I got home, but I knew I had to keep it to myself. If anyone from the team saw it, I'd get my butt whupped big-time.

Six Ways Our Team Could Score a Touchdown
by Scott Hudson, Clueless Sports Reporter

1. Wait until the game is over and the other team has left the field.
2. Get one of our parents to drive the quarterback to the goal line.
3. Let the other team score so many points they feel sorry for us. (This appears to be our actual strategy, but we haven't found the right number yet. It's higher than sixty-three.)
4. Hide a catapult behind the offensive line.
5. Change the rules so you score points every time you get knocked back ten yards or throw the ball away.
6. Buy the points on eBay.

Block that kick.
Block that kick.
Block that writer.

So, this was writer's block. I was completely stuck. Not a clue what to say. Nobody would want to read about the other team. But if I only listed our achievements, the article would be shorter than the headline.

I spent a long time staring at the blank screen on our computer, wishing I'd never written that list of Tom Swifties.

"I have no idea what to write," Scott said thoughtlessly.

I typed a title, deleted it, typed another title, then deleted that.

"I can't possibly write a football article," Scott said unsportingly.

That's when it hit me. The first sentence jumped into my mind. And from my mind to my fingers.

"They keep gaining yards," we said defenselessly.

The next sentence was even easier.

"The first quarter is over and we haven't scored," the crowd yelled pointlessly.

Once I started, it just sort of rolled out.

"Throw the ball," the coach shouted passively.

"We need to keep the ball on the ground," the fullback said dashingly.

I kept it up for the whole article and managed to fit in all the details from the game. It came out pretty good.

{ ten }

*b*_{am.}

Thump.

Pause.

BAM!

Pause.

Thumpa WHUMP!

"Crap."

I pulled the pillow over my head and tried to ignore the crashes and thumps coming from the spare room.

Knock, knock. "Scott?" *Knock, knock, knock.*

I peeked out from beneath the pillow. Mom peeked in from the hall.

"Are you up?" she asked.

"What . . . ?"

"I'm sorry. Did I wake you?" she asked.

"No," I lied, still half asleep. "What's going on?"

"We're clearing out the nursery. Can you take your books?"

"Now?" I looked at my clock. It was barely after eight.

Mom nodded. "Your dad and I have a lot of errands to run later. Please?"

I staggered out of bed and went to the spare room. I'd kept my extra books on some of the shelves made from boards and cinder blocks. It was the only thing I'd ever built. Now the books were piled on the floor and the shelves were disassembled.

"Can't we leave them here?" I asked.

"Cinder blocks?" Mom said, pointing to the floor. "In a nursery?"

Sheesh. What was the baby going to do? Fly out of the crib and crash headfirst into the shelves? Swallow a cinder block? If he could do that, I'd definitely get him a job in a carnival. It would be amazing going in, and twice as amazing coming out. But I could tell it wasn't an area open to discussion. I lugged the books to my room, then tried to go back to sleep, but it was no use. I got up and started on my homework. As I listened to the thumps and crashes coming through the wall, I realized that I was going to be hearing a lot more noise once the nursery got occupied.

Around noon, I knew if I didn't take a break I'd rupture something in my skull. I grabbed the book I was reading for English and headed to the playground at the elementary school to see if the guys were around.

"Hey, it's the lost boy," Patrick said when I got there. He was shooting hoops with Kyle. "Want to play?"

"Sure. For a bit. Is Mitch coming? We could go two-on-two."

"Forget him," Kyle said. "He's gone for good."

"That's just plain wrong," Patrick said. He threw the ball

hard against the backboard, then caught the rebound. "A guy should stick with his friends. No matter what. Right?"

"Right," I said.

Kyle nodded.

"So if there are three of us," Patrick asked, "does that make us the two Musketeers?"

"Something like that," I said.

We played a couple games of H-O-R-S-E. Then I dropped out and let them play one-on-one. I sat on the side of the court and started reading. Right when I was really getting into the story, something whizzed past my face and smacked the book from my hands.

"Are you crazy?" I shouted at Kyle.

"It slipped," he said, giving me a grin as he chased after the basketball.

"No, it didn't," I said.

He scooped up the ball and tossed it to Patrick. "Look, I'm doing you a favor. Trying to save your eyesight. You're going to get all squinty if you keep reading." He scrunched up his eyes and put his hands in front of him like he was trying to feel his way in the dark.

"Very funny." I grabbed my book, moved farther from the court, and sat where I could keep an eye on him while I read.

Later, when they took a break, Patrick actually asked to see the book. He looked at it for a moment, then said, "Doesn't look bad. Probably better than memorizing prepositions."

I nodded. "There's hope for you, after all. Want to read it when I'm done?"

"Nah. I'd rather waste my time on movies and video games."

When Kyle and Patrick knocked off, I headed home. The sweet aroma of warm cake and fresh icing greeted me as I walked past the kitchen.

"What's up?" I asked Mom.

"Bobby got a job," she said.

"Great. Where?"

"The diner on Market Street. It's close enough for him to walk. He starts on Friday."

I guess she'd made the cake to celebrate Bobby's job. Maybe he'd keep this one for a while. "My first article comes out in the school paper on Tuesday," I said.

"That's wonderful."

"I'll show it to you after school."

"That would be nice."

As I pictured her reading the paper, I started to get nervous about my article. Then, as I pictured the whole school reading it, I moved from nervous to terrified. I went upstairs and read it again. Suddenly it didn't seem as hilarious as before. What if people didn't get it? What if it was a truly stupid idea?

I thought about last year's middle school talent show. This seventh grader played the trumpet. He was so bad, the notes could turn your guts to water. But he seemed to think he was great. He didn't have a clue that he was beyond awful. What if that's how it was with my article? Maybe it actually stunk.

I wondered whether I should chuck the whole thing and just write about the game. Something short and simple. *We sucked. We lost.* But I'd already tried, and I hadn't been able to come up with anything else. And it was sort of cool. At least, I hoped it was.

Monday, before homeroom, when I handed in the article, I told Mandy, "It's a little different."

"Excellent." She slipped it into her folder. "No point boring the readers with the same old stuff." She was wearing a long skirt again. With a tight blue top.

"You want to check it to make sure it's okay?"

"I'm sure it will be fine. Good job." She tapped me on the shoulder with the folder, like she was granting me knighthood, then headed down the hall.

Good or bad, it was out of my hands. Nothing much happened in the morning. But then I learned something in the last place I expected. History class. Mr. Ferragamo was telling us about France. We were supposed to be studying ancient Rome, but Mr. Ferragamo tended to get distracted. The Romans had fought the Gauls. And the Gauls later became the French. Once Mr. Ferragamo started explaining this, we ended up smack in the middle of the 1900s. Which was fine, since I could doze as easily there as I could in ancient times. I wasn't alone. Since history was right after lunch, pretty much everyone around me was nodding off, too. As heavy carbs invaded our bloodstreams, heads dropped down and snapped up like we were at some kind of weird prayer meeting. I was napping just fine until he said, "Their leader, during the war years, was Charles de Gaulle."

My eyes opened all the way. *De Gaulle?* That was the same name as my Spanish teacher. Which might not mean anything. But also might explain a lot. I could swear I'd never heard her speak more than a word or two in English. If that much.

I thought about the way she sounded when she taught us. *Hoola sheekoes eee sheekahs, coomo ezdas?* It was almost like she filtered every syllable through her nose. Good grief—she did sound sort of French.

And once, when a kid had tripped over his sneaker laces and fallen flat on his face, she'd shouted, *"Mon dieu!"* As I thought back, that sure seemed pretty French to me.

I knew just how to find out. I waited until seventh period, when I had life skills. Ms. Pell is pretty cool, and she likes to talk. After class, I went up to her desk and asked, "Is Ms. de Gaulle from France?"

"Oh yes," Ms. Pell said. "She came here last year. Good thing for us. There's quite a shortage of qualified Spanish teachers. We were lucky to get her. Lovely lady, though I do admit I sometimes have just a teensy bit of trouble understanding her."

Lucky me. My Spanish teacher spoke mostly French. I guess even her Spanish came out with a French accent. No wonder the stuff she said didn't resemble anything in our book. Great. I was learning a language that virtually nobody else would ever understand. Except for the other kids in the class. I guess you could call it Fanish. Or Spench. Maybe we could start our own country. Our flag would be a huge upside-down question mark.

September 24

Don't ever tell anyone you heard this from me. Okay? But it's something you need to know. There are a lot of good teachers. But some of them don't have a clue. That's the problem. Teachers are just like doctors, plumbers, or painters. Or bus drivers, for that matter. Some are fabulous. Some suck. Most of them are somewhere in the middle. Here—I'll make a list for you.

Scott Hudson's Guide to Teacher Types

The Newbie: Fresh out of teachers' college, she's full of enthusiasm and eager to bond with her students. Newbies are almost always wonderful. Some of them are pretty hot, too.

The Legend: A great teacher. Makes class fun and interesting. Some legends have a gimmick, like they'll wear costumes or play the guitar, or have a famous friend who comes to visit the class.

The Ogre: It's hard to imagine why a person who hates kids would go into teaching. I guess it's some sort of power thing. Or maybe the ogre didn't always hate kids. They come in both male and female varieties. As they age, it becomes very hard to tell them apart.

The Enthusiast: This teacher loves her subject. And she wants you to love it. Her class can be fun, but sometimes she goes way over the students' heads because she knows so much.

The Lifer: He's putting in his time because he couldn't

think of any other way to kill twenty-five or thirty years. Doesn't hate kids. Doesn't like kids. Doesn't really care. He shows up every day and covers the material in the lesson plan, but he could just as well be attaching bolts on an assembly line.

The Lame Duck: A lifer who's about to retire. He has nothing to lose. This can be good since he doesn't give out much work. But it's bad if you want to learn anything.

The Comic: All he wants to do is make the kids laugh. This can be fun if his jokes are any good, or torture if they aren't. The young ones are usually okay. The older ones make jokes about stuff nobody has ever heard of, like old songs and ancient actors.

The Natural: Sometimes, you get someone who just flat-out loves to teach, and is really good at it. No gimmicks. No bad jokes. When you get one, consider yourself lucky.

{ eleven }

Our homeroom teachers passed out the paper Tuesday morning. As soon as I flipped it open, I discovered Mouth had a book review on page 2 of *Revenge of the Mutant Zombies,* a Bucky Wingerton Adventure. He gave it five stars. I almost tossed out the paper when I saw that. Bucky Wingerton books are this cheap series. They churn out a book or two each month. I read one last year, just out of curiosity. It was awful. I doubt there's even a real author. I'd bet they put the books together with some sort of kit. Or a computer program. At least nobody was going to pay any attention to Mouth's review.

My article was on the next-to-last page. I read the whole thing. Which was kind of stupid, I guess, since I was the one who wrote it. But it felt different reading it in the paper. Julia's guest column was in the middle. She'd written about how high school was a great place to make new and interesting friends. She didn't mention anything about long-lost kindergarten pals.

Mr. Franka nodded at me when I walked into English and said, "Good job." Nobody else mentioned my article in any of my classes. I guess mainly because almost nobody knew who I was. I saw Kyle pick the paper up in study hall to look at the cartoons. I wanted to show him my article, but I felt weird about pointing it out. That would be like bragging.

Patrick had the paper with him at lunch. "Not bad," he said when I sat down.

"Thanks." I waited for him to say more, but I guess literary criticism wasn't Patrick's favorite subject. Unfortunately, I quickly discovered someone else who'd read it. Vernon Dross. The varsity quarterback. His loud complaints rumbled at us from the jock table.

"This football stuff sucks," he shouted, tossing down the paper. "It doesn't make any sense."

Great. My writing was getting ripped apart by a guy who moves his lips when he reads a stop sign.

Vernon turned to the kid next to him. "How come he didn't mention my name?"

The kid shrugged, which isn't the best gesture for someone to make when he doesn't have a neck. From behind, it looked like his head was being swallowed by his shoulders.

"I'm the quarterback," Vernon said. "He's supposed to write about me." He jabbed a finger at the paper. "Anybody know this idiot?"

I felt my whole body trying to vanish in a shrug.

They all shook their heads, doing a great imitation of an earthquake at a bobble-head convention. At least my lunch wouldn't be interrupted—or my anatomy rearranged—by an angry quarterback. The team didn't know me, and I wasn't going to do anything to change that.

I brought the paper home, but didn't show it to Mom and

Dad. I was worried that the whole thing with the Tom Swifties was sort of stupid. I'd wait to show them my next article. Bobby was on his way out to work. He'd pulled the four-to-midnight shift at the diner. So I didn't show the article to him, either.

Mom was planning to cook lasagna for dinner, but she got this wild craving for tacos, so Dad and I made a food run.

"School going okay?" he asked as we left the house.

"Yeah. Just fine. How's work?"

"Fine." I looked out the side window for a while, watching the curbs and phone poles fly past.

"This is what your mom does best," Dad said.

"What? Gets cravings?"

"No. Being a mom. She's just so good at it. You should see her with babies."

"I'm pretty sure I will."

"Oh yeah. Right. But it's like she has a magic touch. Babies just melt in her hands."

"We should be so lucky."

"What?"

"Just kidding. What about you? How are you with babies?"

"I managed not to drop either of you."

"Thanks."

September 28

Congratulate me, Smelly. I made it through my first month of high school. No broken bones. No disasters. On the other hand, no hot dates or leaps in popularity either.

I'm pretty sure I carried my middle-school status with

me. Most of us do that, no matter how much we'd like to change. Except Julia. And a few other girls who performed similar metamorphic stunts. (Did you spot the vocabulary word? If you thought I said *metaphoric*, take another look.)

Today Mr. Franka introduced the topic of stream-of-consciousness writing. That's where the writer sort of vomits the contents of his mind onto the page, just letting whatever comes flow out. Go out. Show out the prose and cons and all the twisty little pretzel bends of each thought untaught in the belief that anyone else on the planet would want to read the spewings despite the fact that the writer didn't plan it but just kept going and going like a battery bunny banging a drum like the drum I wanted when I was five but got a toy clarinet instead which broke when I tried to use it to pry up a rock in the backyard next to the apple tree so I could bury my hurt feelings.

Don't feel bad if you skimmed that last sentence. I sure wouldn't read it. I already spend too much time with my streaming, screaming consciousness.

Mr. Franka didn't talk too much about the topic. "You'll get a fair dose of it in college if you forget to duck," he said. "For now, we'll stick with more accessible literature."

Speaking of ducking, my teachers screwed up big-time. None of them gave out any homework. I can relax and enjoy the weekend. Sleep late. Catch a movie with the guys. Oversleep. Shoot some hoops. Get some sleep. All I have to do tonight is cover the game.

I might even go hang around the garage tomorrow. Dad and Bobby are out there now, grinding some sort of cylinder or widget or gasket. Or perhaps it's a brisket.

I saw three kids in the halls carrying *Revenge of the Mutant Zombies.* I'm definitely going to strangle Mouth.

The team got clobbered again. I paid special attention to Vernon, which was like being forced to watch a very bad movie. I needed to mention him a lot in my next story. It wouldn't be easy. He was one of the main reasons the team stank.

At the end of the first quarter, Kyle said, "This really rots."

I glanced over at Patrick. "You aren't even going to make it to halftime, are you?"

He shrugged. "I'll stay if you want me to."

"That's okay," I said. "No reason all three of us should be miserable."

They split. I wished I'd left early, too. Especially when I saw Julia and Kelly walk over to the players' bench and hang out there after the game. Julia spent a lot of time talking with Vernon. I never would have guessed he could hold a conversation. It killed me to see her hovering near him. She was so wonderful and smart. Maybe she was studying him for a science project or something. I sure hoped this wasn't her idea of making new and interesting friends.

When I got home, I went right to work. I didn't want to do more Tom Swifties. That would get old pretty fast. As I thought about the writing I'd been doing recently, I got an idea. Amazingly enough, the second article rolled out as easily as the first.

Once again, I figured I'd sleep late. Obviously, I was slow to learn new lessons. This time, it wasn't thumping that woke me. It was the gentle whisper of a power sander.

Mom, dressed in coveralls with a mask over her nose and mouth, was repainting the spare room. Or the nursery. Or whatever the heck it was going to be.

"What do you think?" Dad asked when I peeked in from the hall. He patted a stack of decals—ducks, bunnies, squirrels, and other lovable critters. But at least, from what I could see, there wouldn't be any Pooh on the wall. At least not yet.

I stared at the plastic wildlife for a moment. "It's nice," I lied. As I left the room, I had a sudden urge to call Uncle Jack and ask him to take me hunting.

September 29
Here's a fact for you. Squirrels are rodents. So are rats. Check out your walls before you go to sleep. Rodents all over. Just figured you'd want to know. But don't worry. They aren't real. At least, not while the lights are on. Who knows what happens in the dark?

And as for flesh-eating ducks—you probably don't even want to hear about them.

I wrote my second article. Check out how it starts:
Dear diary, today I watched Quarterback Vernon Dross and the rest of the Zenger Panthers fight a difficult

battle against the Hoover Hawks. I mentioned Vernon nine times, which should keep him happy. Since guys don't write diaries, I signed it at the end with a made-up girl's name just for fun. The one I came up with was Ema Nekaf. I know it looks kind of fake, but I picked it for a reason. See if you can figure out why. I'll give you a chance to think about it.

I didn't show it to Mom or Dad. They'd probably think it was kind of silly.

Half the kids in school are reading *Revenge of the Mutant Zombies.* I hate Mouth. Strangling is too good for him.

Sunday morning, I heard a crash from downstairs. I figured it was some new remodeling project. Maybe they were installing an indoor wading pool for toddlers.

"Relax. Everything's okay."

It was Mom's voice. She didn't sound okay.

I went down. The coatrack was knocked over. Mom and Dad were hurrying for the garage, jackets in hand.

"What's wrong?"

"Nothing," Mom said. But her face was really pale.

Dad looked like he'd thrown on his clothes real fast. "I'll call and let you know what's going on," he said.

A moment later, they were flying down the street in the Subaru.

Oh man. I went up to Bobby's room and knocked on his door. He didn't answer, so I went in. "Wake up," I said.

He pulled the pillow over his head.

"Come on. Get up." I pushed him on the shoulder.

"Go 'way." He reached out and shoved me.

"Knock it off! This is serious."

"What?" The muffled voice came from under the pillow.

I told him about Mom. When I was done, he sat up, shook his head, and said, "I knew this was a bad idea."

"You think she'll be okay?"

"Yeah. Sure." He reached out and ruffled my hair. It felt weird. Like when you see a cat owner petting a dog.

I went downstairs and straightened up the coatrack, then waited by the phone. I figured Bobby would come down so we could talk. But he didn't. After a while, when I wandered back upstairs, I saw him stuffing clothes in a duffel bag.

"What are you doing?"

"I can't stand this place right now."

"You're leaving?"

"I don't need all this stress. I've got too much stuff to deal with already." He zipped up the bag, then put his guitar in its case. "Got any money?"

"Some."

"Can I borrow it?"

The last thing I wanted was to help him leave. But I figured he'd go no matter what. So I gave him what I had, and he took off for the bus station.

About forty minutes later, Dad called.

"Everything's fine," he said.

"Mom's okay?"

"Yeah. We saw the doctor. We'll be home in a little bit."

"Good."

"How you doing?"

"I'm all right."

I didn't tell him anything else. He'd find out soon enough. I still couldn't believe Bobby had split. He was acting like he was the one whose life was being turned upside down by this. But he was already almost grown up and all. I was the one who had to deal with everything.

September 30

No more screwing around. Okay? Whatever it was you did to send Mom to the doctor, just cut it out. None of us needs that kind of excitement around here. So stop causing trouble. You'll get your chance later.

On top of everything else, Mom got all upset about Bobby splitting. I still can't believe he did it. But he's right about one thing. There's way too much tension around here.

Here's a new word for you. *Flux.* It means "change." Right now, everything is in flux.

You know what? Flux sux.

{ twelve }

trick or treat.

It was only the beginning of October, but when the new girl walked into homeroom, I thought she was made up for Halloween. She'd chopped her hair short and dyed it green. I guess she did it herself. I can't imagine paying anyone for a haircut like that. And she'd stuck pins in her face. Not just earrings or nose rings, though she had plenty of those. She also had studs and barbells and other stuff I don't even know the names of. There was a safety pin jammed through her left eyebrow, and another under her lip. It was kind of freaky.

When she came through the door, it got so quiet you could hear a safety pin drop. I tried not to stare at her. Okay—that's not true. I tried not to let her catch me staring. But I couldn't help myself. I mean, safety pins? There were some kids in school who looked kind of like that, but nobody anywhere near as extreme.

She was wearing a black T-shirt for some band I'd never heard of. It showed a girl crying blood. The girl was clutching a headless teddy bear. Naturally, the bear's neck was also pretty moist. We'd definitely moved far beyond Pooh. This bear more likely had a name like Gush or Spew. My home-room teacher stared at the shirt for a moment, but finally shrugged and looked away.

At lunchtime, I watched the new girl walk into the cafeteria. I would have bet anything she'd head over to the punks, or go to the darkest corner, where the goth batlings sat. Instead, she walked straight to the table by the center window where the popular girls held court. She plunked down, opened up a lunch bag, and started to eat a sandwich. From what I could see, she didn't pay any attention to the evil stares.

As fascinating as all of this was, I had something far more important on my mind. Survival. The paper had come out that morning.

"You're acting like there's a bug in your burger," Patrick said.

"Huh?" I glanced down. I'd been gripping it hard enough to leave holes in the bun, but hadn't taken a bite yet. I kept checking Vernon's table, waiting for him to start shouting. But I didn't hear any complaints. I guess I could cross that worry off my list.

I sighed and took a bite. "Government regulations actually allow a certain quantity of insect parts in food," I said.

"Thanks a lot." Kyle dropped his burger onto his tray. "Another thing I didn't need to know. I'm happy being ignorant."

Patrick shrugged. "Good source of protein."

At least things were quiet at home. Though it was weird walking along the hall upstairs. Bobby's room was on one side of mine. Smelly's was on the other. Both empty. Meet the Hudson kids—one had split, one hadn't arrived, and the other didn't have a clue about where he was going.

Dad spent a lot of time in the garage working on the 'vette, even though Bobby wasn't around to give him a hand. I hung out there when I had a chance, though I mostly just watched Dad, or read. Sometimes, he'd look over to his left, like he was going to ask Bobby to pass him a wrench.

Whenever he asked me to hand him a tool, it took me about three tries to find the right one.

Once in a while, Dad would point to some part of the engine and explain what he was doing. I'd nod and try to say something that showed I was interested. Once in a while, I'd hold up my book and explain about some cool part I'd just read. Dad would nod and say, "That's interesting." I didn't offer to read to him. That didn't feel like a guy thing.

Mom was worried about Bobby, but he'd called when everyone was out and left a message saying he was visiting friends in Ohio, so at least we knew where he was. Dad had already stopped by the diner to let them know Bobby wouldn't be showing up for work.

In school, the halls started to fill up with hand-lettered posters. Five kids were running for freshman-class president. Including Julia. The other candidates were dorks, so there was no way she'd lose.

Maybe she could do something about crime when she got elected. After being careful for nearly a month, I forgot to wrap up my change in my backpack. Just when I realized my pocket was jingling, Wesley Cobble approached me for a donation.

I'm not a complete wimp, and it's not like I'll never stand up for myself, but Wesley is flat-out scary. He isn't the biggest kid in the school. A lot of the football players are bigger. The thing is, he has this look in his eyes like he really doesn't care what happens to him. There's no way to predict how he'll react to something. If I told him he couldn't have my change, he might just shrug and walk off. Or he might punch me and kick me until there was nothing left but painful memories and calcium dust.

I wish I could lock Wesley and Vernon in a room and let them destroy each other. At the moment, all I could do was try to avoid him, and make a note on the subject for the benefit of others. I pulled out my notebook and wrote a quick list. The funny thing is that by the time I was finished, I felt a lot better.

Scott Hudson's Guide for Spotting Unpredictable People
1. They have dried blood on their clothes.
2. Their tattoos are scarier than most horror movies.
3. They ask questions for which there is no safe answer, like "What are you looking at?"
4. They tend not to have a huge circle of friends.

Patrick, on the other hand, remained painfully predictable. He was always trying to talk me into stuff. "You should run," he said, pointing to the student-council sign-up sheet on the bulletin board.

"You've got to be crazy," I said.

"Hey, I'm serious. There are just eight kids signed up for council. And three spots. You'd have a chance."

"No, I wouldn't. The whole thing is a popularity contest. Even if I did have a chance, why in the world would I want to be on the student council? I don't even know what they do."

Patrick grinned at me. "Because the council meets with the class president."

I tried not to let my face show that I'd taken a shot to the gut. "What are you talking about?"

"I'm not blind. I see you drooling whenever Julia moves into sight. I can hear your heart beat from the other side of the building. Can't blame you. She's pretty hot."

"No way. I'm just . . ."

Patrick stared right at me, still grinning. I couldn't lie to him. "God, is it that obvious?"

He shrugged. "I doubt anyone else around here cares whether your tongue is hanging out. Except maybe the guy who cleans the floors."

A thought hit me, along with a second blow to the stomach. "You think Kyle noticed?" I could see him torturing me with that information. Or maybe torturing Julia with it. Or—oh, my God—mentioning it to Vernon just for fun. When we were little, it was always Kyle who did the worst damage to anthills and spiderwebs.

"Not a chance. He's too busy noticing himself."

"Yeah, I guess. Look. It's no big deal. I think she's cute. But there are plenty of cute girls. A whole school full of them. And she doesn't even notice me, anyhow. It's really nothing."

Patrick tapped the board. "Your choice. But if it was me, I'd go for it. What do you have to lose?"

October 3
I decided to run for student council. I think it could be an interesting experience. After all, what have I got to lose?

I finished *The Outsiders.* It was good. Started reading *Ender's Game.* Another weird title. Which, as we've seen, might promise good things to come.

Oh, you probably figured out Ema Nekaf by now. If not, read it backward.

Friday morning, I was walking into the building with Mouth when I saw Wesley strolling down the hall. I slowed up and let Mouth get ahead. He didn't even seem to notice that I wasn't there. He just kept walking and talking.

When Wesley reached him, they had a brief conversation. Then Mouth handed over his money. I stepped into a classroom and waited until Wesley went past. On the way down the hall, I saw Mouth at his locker. I almost kept going, but I felt sort of bad for him.

"Need lunch money?" I asked.

"Yeah, I guess I do. How'd you know? I had money, but I ran into this guy who asked me for some, and my mom always says it's better to give than receive, so I figured that was what I should do. But maybe not, because doesn't that mean that the other guy is receiving? So it's not better for him. Right?"

I handed him a couple bucks. He followed me down the hall all the way to homeroom and kept thanking me. I was glad I didn't give him more. He probably would have asked if we could become blood brothers.

Later, he even came over to our lunch table and sat down so he could thank me some more and show me how wisely he'd used my money.

"Seat's taken," Kyle said, cutting into Mouth's monologue.

Mouth moved to another seat. I glanced across to the popular girls' table. The new kid with the green hair was sitting there again. I guess girls handle things differently than guys.

"That one's taken, too," Kyle said.

Mouth got up. "No problem. I don't have time to hang out right now, anyhow. I have to work on my speech. How's yours coming, Scott?"

My gut clenched with a ripple of panic as I wondered whether I'd forgotten about a homework assignment. "What speech?"

"For student council. You know, we have to make a speech next Tuesday. All the candidates."

"Are you serious?" I'd never given a speech.

Mouth nodded.

I looked over at Patrick. "Did you know about this?"

He shrugged. "Why should I? I'm not running."

Oh man. I tried to picture myself standing in front of the whole class. I felt like someone was kneeling on my throat.

"What's going on?" Kyle asked.

"Scott's running for student council," Patrick said.

Kyle snorted.

"So am I," Mouth said. "Which is good. Because you get three votes. So you can vote for me and Scott, and still have a vote left over for someone else."

"Going to the game tonight?" I asked Kyle, in a desperate effort to change the subject.

"No way. I've given up on that."

I wish I could have given up on football. But I had no choice. Worse, it was an away game. I rode there after school with the band. I could have gone on the players' bus, but that would have been suicide. I didn't even want to think about riding there with a bunch of psyched-up jocks. Or riding home with them after they'd lost.

And lose, we did. Big-time.

October 5
Remember how I hoped *Ender's Game* would be good? Well, it was beyond that. I could hardly put it down. I read more than half the book the night I started it. I just finished it on the bus ride back from the game. I know Mouth would like it, but it would kill me to see him review it. I think Patrick would like it, too. I've tried getting him interested in books before, but it just doesn't

work. I guess I can sort of understand that. I used to be the same way. Until a while ago, I wasn't interested in books. It all changed by accident.

When I crashed my bike and broke my arm, back in fifth grade, I was banged up enough that I had to spend a couple days in the hospital. There was this other kid in the room. Tobie. He was always reading. One book right after another. He didn't even look at the television. The third day, after he'd finished this book, he started talking about how it was the best thing he'd ever read. He kept bugging me to read it. I figured he wanted us to have something to talk about.

So I read it. But not really. I skimmed it, like I did in school. I held it so I could see the TV over the top—not easy with one arm in a cast—and made sure I didn't turn the pages too quickly.

The instant I closed the book, he was all over me. "Did you like it? It's good, huh? What was your favorite part?"

"It was great. What was your favorite part?" I faked my way through the discussion. Mostly, I let him talk. I don't know if he caught on. It didn't matter. He seemed happy. I went home the next day.

A month later, this box came in the mail. It was from Tobie. Actually, from his folks, because he'd died. But he'd told them he wanted me to have some of his books since we'd become such good friends at the hospital. For a week, I couldn't bring myself to open the box. Or even touch it. But I had to read those books. And I did. Every single one. I didn't skip a word.

They were great.

I've been reading books ever since.

Here are some of the books that were in the box:

Sideways Stories from the Wayside School

The Adventures of Sherlock Holmes

Jeremy Thatcher, Dragon Hatcher

Charlie and the Chocolate Factory

Hatchet

A Spell for Chameleon

Dragonflight

Tuck Everlasting

5,000 Amazing Facts

Yup. I read 5,000 facts. I know all sorts of things nobody else cares about. Except you. You're going to be interested in everything I tell you, whether you like it or not. Sorry. You don't get a choice.

Enough. I'm going to sleep. And I don't plan to wake up for a good long time.

Horses can sleep standing up, by the way. So can freshmen. No lie.

I ended up writing the article like it was a speech. *My fellow spectators, why are we here, and what do we want? I'll tell you. We're here to watch football, and we want touchdowns.* Which is fine for an article that nobody is going to read, but wouldn't be all that great for a real speech. Everything I came up with sounded stupid.

Hi, I'm Scott. Please vote for me.

My name is Scott Hudson, and I need your vote.

Hi, friends . . .

Crap. Stupid popularity contest. What was the point? Nobody would vote for me. Even though they had three votes.

Wait. Three votes . . . That was it. I chucked what I'd written, and started something new.

{ thirteen }

I'm Scott Hudson. I'm running for student council. I know two things for sure. Most of you have no idea who I am. And all of you are going to vote for your friends. So I don't have a chance. With nine kids running, I'd probably come in tenth."

They laughed at my joke, which I took as a good sign. I needed all the encouragement I could get. As it was, I had so much sweat dripping down my hand that I'd expected to be electrocuted when the principal passed me the microphone. The only thing that kept me going was hearing how pathetic some of the other speeches were. One kid even did his as a poem. A truly sucky poem. I was pretty sure *vote* didn't rhyme all that well with *thought*. And I was positive *student* and *you bet* didn't rhyme at all.

Another kid promised to try to get free ice cream at lunch and no homework on Fridays. Good luck. Actually, I guess you could promise to *try* to do anything. I could have promised to try to replace gym class with Victoria's Secret fashion shows.

I finished my speech with what I hoped was a stroke of brilliance. "Even if you have no idea who I am, you get three votes. I'd bet that most of you don't have more than two friends running for student council. So I'm going to ask you to give me that third vote. Who knows? Maybe I'll bring some fresh ideas to the student council. Thank you."

They even clapped when I was done. Sort of. Either that, or the gym had just been invaded by a half-dozen mosquitoes.

For all his talk about getting prepared, Mouth didn't seem to have a speech ready. He just rambled along until they told him his time was up.

Julia's speech, on the other hand, was great. She seemed so calm and confident.

My public-speaking efforts didn't attract any more attention than my writing. Nobody who didn't already know me said anything to me in the halls. Well, I'd given it a shot. And at least I hadn't written my speech as a sucky poem. Elections were in a week. Guess I'd find out then how my idea worked.

In one of those weird coincidences, Mr. Franka started out class the next day by saying, "How many of you don't like poetry?"

Many hands went up. Including mine.

He passed an open book to Vicky Estridge. "Read that out loud."

She started reading this poem about a guy freezing to death up in the Yukon. It was pretty cool. Mr. Franka grabbed another book and handed it to Julia. She read a short, funny poem about a pelican. Then I got to read one called "On the Naming of Cats." I liked it.

After we'd heard three or four more poems, Mr. Franka

said, "There are as many types of poems as there are types of food. As many flavors, you might say. To claim you don't like poetry because you hate 'mushy stuff' or things you don't immediately understand is like saying you hate food because you don't like asparagus."

He looked around the room again. "So, who can at least tolerate poetry?"

All the hands went up.

"Let's visit Xanadu." He gave us a page number in our textbooks. "Read 'Kubla Khan' to yourself. Listen to the music. Let Coleridge speak to you."

I started reading, and was hooked by the fourth line.

Mr. Franka read us another poem, called "To Augusta." This one was sort of mushy, but even so the words sounded pretty cool. They flowed, like good music.

"Byron," Mr. Franka said, closing the book. "You've all heard his work, whether you realize it or not. 'She walks in beauty, like the night.' You can't tell me that line doesn't kick butt. Byron even wrote a poem filled with ghosts and vampires."

That caught my attention. Before I could ask about the poem, he said, "I won't tell you the name. If you really want to find it, you'll have to hunt it down. Or should I say, haunt it down?"

From there, he skipped around to some of his other favorite poets. Not once during the whole class did Mr. Franka utter those deadly words, "Now, what does this line mean?" He actually let us enjoy the poems without analyzing them to death. As he told us, sometimes a dying snake is just a dying snake. Sometimes a leafless tree is just a tree.

At the end of the period, he said, "April is national poetry month. That's why we're reading poetry in October."

I couldn't resist. I raised my hand and asked, "So what are we going to study in April?"

He flashed a smile at me, and I felt doom approaching. I knew that smile. It's the one you get when a fish that's been nibbling at your bait for five minutes finally gulps it down. "Thank you, Scott."

"What for?"

"I usually let the first person who asks that question make the decision about what to study in April. Congratulations. Ladies and gentlemen, we have a winner. Let me know your choice by mid-March."

Great. Just what I need—a chance to get an entire English class pissed at me. At least the typical honors English student was a bit less threatening than the typical defensive lineman.

October 11

Check this out, Smelly:

In Xanadu did Kubla Khan
A stately pleasure-dome decree:
Where Alph, the sacred river, ran
Through caverns measureless to man
Down to a sunless sea.

Stop. Go back. Read it again. Read it out loud. Listen to the words. Hear the words. I hope you get what I'm talking about. I just love the phrase "caverns measureless to man." That's genius. I mean, I would have said something lame like "really big caves."

I think I like poetry. There's an awful lot of it out there. And there's a lot of it that's awful. But there's also a ton that's good. And a lot that goes way beyond good.

Dad can hear when an engine isn't running right. Bobby can hear when his guitar is even slightly out of tune. I can't do that, but I think I can hear when a poem is good. Or a sentence.

Go, team, go.

Yeah, right.

Another Friday, another football game. Our team scored a touchdown. The crowd was so surprised, nobody even cheered. Their mouths just hung open like measureless caverns. The other team scored eleven times. Final score, 76 to 7. They should have had seventy-seven, but they missed one of the extra points. Not because of our defense. I think their kicker was getting tired. It was hard to tell for sure from up in the stands, but I suspect he might also have been laughing so hard it threw off his aim.

I figured I could concentrate on our small moment of glory for my article. Since it took us thirteen plays to get down the field, I'd have plenty to write about. I didn't want to think about any other part of the game. Julia spent the whole second half standing by the fence behind the players' bench.

Kyle didn't come, but Patrick hung out for a while.

I played around with doing the article as a poem, but it didn't feel right. I wasn't worried. I had extra time since we'd get Monday off for Columbus Day. I ended up writing it like it was an infomercial for the greatest hits of the Zenger Panthers. I was pretty happy with the way it came out.

We voted on Tuesday in homeroom. It felt weird to vote for myself. Sort of like cheating. Kyle and Patrick voted for me, too. So did Mouth. He told me so. Five times. Maybe six. That is—he told me five times. He didn't vote five times. But even if he had, it wouldn't make a difference. I voted for him. But I didn't tell him.

On the way out of homeroom, the new girl—her name was Lee—said, "Your speech moved me to tears. I voted for you. You owe me ten dollars." She held her hand out.

I stared at the black fishnet sleeve that covered her arm.

"Duh," she said. "Joking."

She turned and walked off before I could say anything clever.

"Good luck," Patrick said at the end of the day.

"Thanks. But I don't have a prayer."

"Come on. You've got to at least kind of think that you could possibly win."

"I guess." Maybe he was right. Even though I knew for sure that I wouldn't win, I also sort of thought I might. It didn't make

sense, but that's how it was. Everyone who was running probably thought the same thing. Which meant six of us were wrong.

I'd find out soon enough.

October 17
I hope you're sitting down. I mean, sitting down when
you read this. Right now, I guess you're floating. I wonder
if you can blow bubbles? Ick.

Anyhow, here's the shocking news. I won. My speech
worked. I'm a student-council member. Can you believe
that? It would be great, except that Julia lost. I made it
and she didn't. I'll bet you saw that coming. You're
probably laughing your head off at me while you're
reading this. Your squishy, transparent, fishlike head with
beady little black dots for eyes.

Mouth lost. He only got three votes. But he came right
up to me and said, "Congratulations." That's a shortened
version.

I wanted to tell Julia that I was sorry she'd lost. But I
figured she wouldn't want to be reminded of it. Especially
by someone who won. Oh crap—I didn't even think about
that. I probably just killed any chance I had. Not that I
had a chance. Though I sort of thought I did, even though
I know I don't. Like I thought I had a chance to win the
election.

Friday afternoon, I could see Patrick's grin from all the way
down the hall.

"Now what?" I asked when I reached him and Kyle.

"We have to go," he said.

I looked at the poster he was pointing to. There was a harvest dance next week, right after the game. "No way."

"You have to go," Kyle said. "Unless you're planning to spend the next four years with your nose in a book."

"No argument," Patrick said. "We're going. It's for your own good. Someday, you'll thank us for dragging you out into the world."

I reached inside my backpack. "I'll tell you what. While we're doing each other favors, let me do one for you." I handed him my copy of *Ender's Game*.

"What's this?" he asked.

"Just read it. Trust me."

"Weird title."

"That's not a bad thing."

"I'm sort of busy."

"With what? You told me you aren't getting much homework. Just give it a try. Okay?"

He shrugged. "I'll see."

"What about the game tonight? You going?"

He shook his head. "I think I'd rather read a book."

Back at home, I found myself facing another interesting weekend. Mom suddenly realized that we didn't live in a house—we lived in a baby-mauling machine. My God, the horrors that surrounded us. Electricity running through the walls. The horror! Deadly poisons behind the cabinets. Beware! Sharp tools.

Heavy objects. Zillions of plastic bags. Mold spores by the billion! It's a wonder Bobby and I survived the sharp-edged, smothering, high-voltage death trap we called home.

Mom went on a mission to remedy the situation. She drafted Dad to help. I suspect that eventually there'll be nothing in the house except foam-rubber furniture and rodent decals.

October 20

Hey, you awake in there? Got a question for you. I've been trying to figure something out. Sadly, you're the only entity who's available at the moment. Anyhow, here's the question. I'm thinking about doing my next article as a series of couplets. They're easy to write. It's just two lines that rhyme. Like, if you were describing one of our football games, you could say:

We had the ball.
Not at all.

Sometimes, a couplet has a title that's longer than the poem.

Our Quarterback's Strategy for Finding a Receiver
He threw each pass
Right at the grass.

You get the idea. And don't worry, I'm smart enough not to write anything that will get me in trouble. Like:

A Brief History of Panther Touchdowns

Vernon
Didn't earn 'em.

So what do you think? Good idea? Bad idea? Send me a message. Kick once for *yes* and twice for *no.* Wait, I forgot, you probably don't have any muscles yet. Or feet.

Oh, ick,
You can't kick.

{ fourteen }

Monday, in English, Mr. Franka said, "My friends, allow me to introduce you to Percy Bysshe Shelley."

After we'd stopped laughing at his name, we spent the period reading his poems. While I wasn't super thrilled by his stuff, Mr. Franka mentioned that his wife, Mary Wollstonecraft Shelley, wrote *Frankenstein.* He also told us that the two of them were friends with Byron. And they all hung out with this other guy named Polidori, who'd written a vampire story. Now I knew I had to get my hands on that ghost poem.

Tuesday, we studied haiku. Wednesday, we got our school pictures. I had no idea that my hair was that weird after gym class. I looked like a chipmunk. Mom went all gooey when she saw the picture, like she doesn't see me live and in person every single day. But she'd been pretty emotional the last couple weeks. She cried a lot when she watched movies on TV. Even during funny shows. I think there's more going on inside her than Dad and I will ever understand.

I got cornered by Mouth on Thursday at the bus stop. "Hey, ready for the dance?" he asked.

I glanced over at Julia and tried to think of some reply that would lure her into the conversation. But Mouth didn't leave me an opening.

"What are you planning to wear? I bought a new shirt. It's got stripes, so it makes me look taller. Girls like tall guys. Your brother is real tall, isn't he? I don't know if I should wear shoes or sneakers. What are you wearing?" He actually paused long enough for me to slip in an answer.

"Sneakers," I told him.

"That's what I thought. But what if everyone else is wearing shoes? Maybe I can put a pair of shoes in my locker. Extra shirts, too. Because I sweat a lot. Mom says I have a fast metabolism. I go through deodorant like crazy. I tried a roll-on, but I think a stick works better for me. I don't want to use a spray because you can breathe it in, which is a big waste since lungs don't sweat, right? I mean, there's no way they could, because then we'd all drown. Imagine that. Drowning in your own sweat."

At that point, I stopped listening and passed the time composing couplets. Such as:

Me dance?
Fat chance.

I went to the dance right from the game. I wore old sneakers and an old shirt. It didn't matter. I could have dressed in a tux or wrapped myself in aluminum foil. The result would still have been the same. Patrick, Kyle, and I stood near the wall the whole time, drinking store-brand soda and eating those really cheap potato chips—the ones that are so thin you can read through them and so greasy they almost slip out of your fingers.

We had a contest to see who could whistle first after eating a handful of chips. We usually did that with crackers, but sometimes you need to improvise. Patrick won. The floor lost.

As I looked around the gym, I had this scary thought that I couldn't help sharing. "What if this is as good as it gets? We might look back years from now and think how great life was when we were freshmen."

Patrick shook his head. "Don't say that. It has to get better."

Kyle glared at Mitch, who was dancing with his girlfriend. "Hey, if a loser like him can get a girl, so can I."

I nodded as a show of support, but didn't bother to lie out loud.

None of us danced. We just kept pushing one another and saying, "Ask her." "No, you ask her." "No, *you* ask her."

Mouth actually asked a bunch of different girls to dance. It was painful to watch. The scene reminded me of a bee trapped in a window. He'd buzz over and explore a spot, discover there was no opening, drop back and hover for a while, then try another spot. The bees never find a way out. Their dried corpses litter the windowsills.

But maybe I shouldn't feel sorry for him. He didn't seem to feel any pain. In a way, he was better off than the rest of us.

Julia was there. Dancing with Vernon. She was a great dancer. Vernon, on the other hand, moved like a cardboard robot from a really cheap science-fiction movie. When I watched them together, I felt like someone was cutting small holes in my lungs with a sharp knife.

Saturday afternoon, Patrick called to tell me he was halfway through the book and really enjoying it.

Sunday, he called again.

"Finish the book?" I asked. I wondered what to give him next.

"Yeah."

"Wasn't it great?"

"Yup."

He sounded weird. "What's wrong?"

"We're moving."

"Where?"

"Texas. My dad got transferred. We're leaving next month."

"Crap. That's halfway across the country."

"Yeah. Crap."

October 29

I tried something different. I wrote about the football game in the form of a play.

The dance was pretty awful. I'm not doing that again.

This is stupid. I don't want to talk about my article or the dance. What I want is to punch my wall real hard. A bunch of times. I can't believe Patrick is moving. We've been friends since second grade. That's like almost my whole life. He can't leave. It's not right. How can his dad do this to him? All parents ever do is screw things up for their kids.

···

"Take arms against a sea of troubles," Mr. Franka said. He always paced in front of us when he recited stuff, as if the power of the words gave him so much energy he couldn't stand still. "Recognize it?"

A bunch of us said, "Shakespeare."

"Right. But think about that line. 'Take arms against a sea of troubles.' Anyone troubled by it?"

I'd heard that line a bunch of times, but I'd always let the words run through my brain without examining them. Now I saw the problem. I was pretty sure that *arms* meant weapons or battle or something like that. Why would you take weapons against a sea of anything? It didn't make sense.

As I sat there deep in thought, Julia raised her hand. "It doesn't make sense," she said.

"Exactly!" Mr. Franka increased his pacing speed. "It's what we call a mixed metaphor. In Shakespeare's case, he can pull it off. But lesser writers can really drop the ball. Or, to use a mixed metaphor, they can fumble the beans."

He gave us a couple more examples, then asked us to come up with some of our own. Toward the end of class, he said, "In a similar vein, we have oxymorons. Words that seem to contradict each other. *Jumbo shrimp* is a classic example. Those are words that just don't belong together."

Like Julia and Vernon, I thought. They definitely didn't belong together. Mr. Franka might be able to explain all about language, but I needed to take this particular issue to a different expert.

"Why do girls go out with jerks?" I asked Mom when I got home from school.

"Lots of reasons. Maybe they don't think the boy is a jerk. Or maybe they're just going through their bad-boy stage."

"Bad-boy stage?" That didn't sound encouraging.

"Don't worry. Most of them grow out of it. And then they'll notice there are nice boys like you to date."

"How long does that take?"

"It depends. Not long for the smart girls."

Well, that, at least, was a glimmer of hope. Julia was definitely smart. Not that she'd leap into my arms if she left Vernon. At least, not outside my dreams.

October 31

Happy Halloween. I can't wait to dress you up in a costume. A mummy would be cool. It would be a good chance for me to practice my fishing knots. Of course, that's assuming Mom doesn't go for something a bit cuter. Either way, there are only two things you need to remember. Number one—share your candy.

Number two—I get first choice.

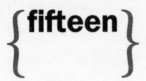

{ **fifteen** }

he's trying to kill us," I gasped. Bits of frost coated my words as they left my mouth.

"Cold air is good for us," Kyle said.

"Maybe if we were TV dinners." I couldn't believe Mr. Cravutto was still dragging the class outside. "Doesn't he own a calendar? Or a thermometer?"

I wasn't the only one complaining. Nearly everyone tried to point out to Mr. Cravutto that the weather had turned slightly brisk. He didn't care. He stood there and shouted, "Suck it up, babies. Make your own heat! Come on, *hustle!*"

I wondered what it felt like to have sweat freeze on your face. I had a sinking suspicion I was going to find out. All I could think about was those Jack London stories where people were stuck in the Yukon wilderness as the temperature plunged to forty below zero. I really didn't want my toes to break off. Or my nose. If that made me a big baby, I could live with it.

Mom and Dad spent most of the weekend shopping for a mobile to hang over the crib. They hadn't bought a crib yet, but the logic and order of their purchases was just another of the many mysteries of birth.

Monday, after school, I went to my first student-council meeting. All we did was talk about ways to improve school spirit. I tried to suggest some ideas, but the older kids completely ignored the freshmen. This did little for our spirit.

Tuesday, life took an unusual twist. Everyone has something he checks out. Dad's interested in cars. Mom notices babies. Ever since Kyle got a Rolex watch from his rich grandfather last year, he's always looking at people's wrists. Patrick knows every brand and style of sneaker. The way he walks around gazing at feet, he's going to end up with a bent neck.

As for me, if I see anyone carrying a book, I try to spot the title and author. It's always nice when someone's reading something you like. Though half the time I look at books now, I end up staring at whatever junk Mouth just reviewed.

On the way out of homeroom, I noticed that Lee was carrying a paperback. I didn't recognize it. I sped up and glanced at the book as I went by, figuring I could do it without her noticing. I'd expected something really dark, like Anne Rice or H. P. Lovecraft. Instead, peeking out at me from the front cover, I saw the name S. Morgenstern. I was so surprised, I stopped walking.

I guess she noticed I was staring. Which she should be pretty used to, what with the pins in her face, the green hair, the eight pounds of mascara, the weird shirts, and all.

I didn't want her to think I was staring at her face or clothes or anything, so I pointed to the book and said, "Morgenstern . . ." One of the best books ever is *The Princess Bride*. It's by William Goldman. The cool thing is, the book itself is supposed to be about a book that Goldman read when he was a kid. So Goldman made up this author, S. Morgenstern. As far as I knew, the only book "written" by S. Morgenstern was *The Princess Bride*.

It's always great to find out that a favorite author has a book you didn't know about. It's like thinking you finished your soda but then you grab the can and there's still some left. Only it's a thousand times better.

She held up the cover. *The Silent Gondoliers: A Fable by S. Morgenstern.* "You like Goldman?"

I nodded. Now that we were face-to-face, I really didn't want to start a conversation. Ick—I think she'd just gotten another ring in her nose. Not that I kept count. If civilization ever broke down, she could probably survive for months by bartering all that metal for food.

"You like *The Princess Bride*?" she asked.

I shrugged.

"Ah, I see you're the strong, silent type."

While I was trying to think of something to say, or some way to avoid saying anything, she tucked the book under her arm and headed down the hall. On the back of her shirt, in a sea of black, a yellow pair of Cheshire-cat eyes, hovering above a smug smile, stared at me.

Later that afternoon, between sixth and seventh period, she glanced toward me as we passed in the hall. I sort of nodded, out of reflex. But I hurried away. I didn't want her to start talking to me. She was just too weird.

• • •

November 7

It's weird. I've known Julia since I was little. But we drifted in different directions. When we pass each other in the hall, she never even looks at me. I've sort of nodded at her a couple times, but they were the small nods a guy uses when he isn't sure he's going to get anything in return.

What would have happened if we'd stayed friends? Would she have dumped me when she turned gorgeous? I'd like to think not, but I have no idea. I guess I really don't know anything about her except that she's beautiful and smart. Does that make me shallow? I don't care. I want her to notice me. I want her to like me and laugh at my jokes and walk down the street holding my hand. I hope I figure some of this stuff out. Not just for your sake, Smelly. For mine, too.

Oh great. It just hit me. You're going to be exactly like Bobby, with girls following you all around and everything. I'll get to watch it again. No. I'm not going to wimp out. We've read all these poems in English about guys who worshipped someone from afar and never spoke up. No way that's happening to me.

Tomorrow morning, I'm going to say hi to Julia. That's all. I'll just walk up to her at the bus stop and say hi. There's no reason not to.

If "music hath charms to soothe a savage breast," then why are there so many hyperactive geeks in the band? I'd caught a ride to the game with them again. It wasn't bad until the bus broke down on the way back. They all took out their instruments and started playing Sousa marches while we waited for the school to send another bus.

I expected them to start thrusting woodwinds at me and screaming, "Join us!"

The marches didn't lift my spirits. I was still angry with myself for not saying hi to Julia that morning. I'd almost done it, but then I'd lost my nerve. I still couldn't understand how Mouth could walk up to anyone in the world and just start talking.

The whole day was pretty much a disaster. Until I started working on my article. That was fun. I borrowed an idea from English class. Last week, we'd read this story called "The Waltz," by Dorothy Parker. Mr. Franka told us a lot about her. She was a master of sarcasm. Someone once asked her, "Do you mind if I smoke?" She replied, "I don't care if you burn."

In "The Waltz," the reader hears what this woman is thinking, and then what she's saying. Nothing else. She's talking to this guy who's asked her to dance. Everything she says is polite, but then you find out what she thinks. And what she thinks is far from nice. It's a brilliant story. Reading something like that for the first time is an amazing experience.

Dorothy Parker also wrote book reviews. I should be so lucky.

Saturday, I went to the garage for advice. Dad was under the 'vette, so I had a conversation with his legs.

"How long did it take before you finally talked to Mom?"

"A couple months."

"How come it took so long?"

"I didn't want to say the wrong thing."

"So, what'd you say to her?"

"Hi."

"That's it. Just hi?"

"Sure. It's about the easiest thing there is to say. Especially when you're nervous. Besides, it worked, didn't it?"

Monday morning, I decided it was time for that act of bravery. Julia was already at the bus stop. I figured I'd flash her the Hudson smile and say, "Hi, Julia," then walk past. That's all. Smile and say hi. It was a start.

This time, my courage held. I moved toward her. Oh God, she was beautiful. I opened my mouth. And made sounds. The syllables shifted across several broken octaves, creating a noise that was somewhere between the creak of an ancient door hinge and the gasp an asthmatic kid makes when he gets punched in the gut.

My voice was changing.

Julia glanced toward me, frowning as if she was trying to make sense out of the noise. I forced my gaze straight ahead and sped past, praying that she didn't realize the pathetic purpose of my croaking.

"Even you can't think this is a good idea." I stood next to Kyle, shivering.

"It's just flurries," he said. "No big deal."

"Suck it up, babies!" Mr. Cravutto shouted.

There had to be some sort of state law against this. He got to stand around in a sweatsuit and a jacket, with his hands in his pockets, while we shivered and tried to "make our own heat." On the other hand, if I froze to death, I wouldn't have to run my failed conversation with Julia through my mind another six million times.

After calisthenics, we played touch football. Now I knew why they called it a huddle. We all huddled together for warmth. Well, as much as guys can huddle.

"This is crazy," I said when we headed into the locker room.

Kyle stared at me. "Hey, your voice is changing."

"I noticed."

Tuesday was Patrick's last day. "I'll come over for a while," I told him when we were heading toward our buses.

He shook his head. "Everything's packed. We're leaving as soon as I get home."

"So, like, you're gone?"

"Yeah. I guess I'm gone."

Across the lot, my bus was almost loaded. I knew the shouter wouldn't wait for me. "We'll keep in touch," I said as I dashed off.

"Right." Patrick waved. "I'll e-mail you when we get unpacked."

As I got on the bus, I realized I might never see him again.

{ sixteen }

I happened to walk past Lee's table at lunch. She had this book of Byron's poems. I figured if anyone knew stuff about vampires, it would be her. "You like him?" I asked.

"Big fan," she said.

"Do you know any vampire poem he wrote?"

A couple of the girls at the table frowned at me with the same sort of annoyed look you'd give a horsefly approaching a bowl of potato salad. I figured I should leave. I really didn't want to get into any sort of long conversation with her, anyhow. Before I could move, Lee grinned and started reciting lines of verse in a voice barely above a whisper:

> *"But first, on earth as Vampire sent,*
> *Thy corse shall from its tomb be rent:*
> *Then ghastly haunt thy native place,*
> *And suck the blood of all thy race;*
> *There from thy daughter, sister, wife,*
> *At midnight drain the stream of life;*
> *Yet loathe the banquet which perforce*
> *Must feed thy livid living corse . . ."*

I could feel the hairs on the back of my neck stand at attention. What an amazing poem. It was wonderfully creepy. As she finished the last line, she plucked a french fry from her tray and licked a glob of ketchup off the tip. There was a stud piercing her tongue. It was shaped like a tiny skull. Past her, the popular girls were completely ignoring us now. Great. I guess they'd lumped me in with Lee as somebody to avoid.

"*Corse* means *corpse,* of course," she said. "But you probably figured that out."

I glanced around to make sure nobody else was watching us talk. "Is that the whole poem?"

"No way. It's huge."

"What's it called?"

She told me the name. It sounded like "The Jawer." I pointed at the book. "Is it in there?" I was dying to read the rest of it.

"Nope. But I have it at home. Want me to bring it in?"

I had this image of her handing me a solid black book with pins stuck in the cover. And maybe a bit of dried blood crusted on the pages. "No thanks."

"You sure?"

"Yeah. Thanks anyhow."

When I got to our table, Kyle snickered and said, "Learning witchcraft from Weirdly?" That's what everyone called her. Weird Lee.

"Had to ask her about an algebra assignment," I lied.

Kyle made a kissing sound, then grabbed his lip and said, "Ouch. Those damn pins."

"Screw you." I threw a bag of chips at him.

"Thanks." He opened them and crammed a handful in his mouth, munched for a while, then said, "They ever put in a metal detector, she's not getting past the front door."

"They ever put in a fart detector, you'll be standing outside, too." I added a sound effect to drive home my point.

Kyle threw the chips back at me, which was part of my crafty plan, except that half of them flew from the bag.

The moment I got home, I tried to find the poem online, but I didn't have a clue how to spell the title. I tried *Jawer, Jour, Jore,* and a bunch of other stuff. After a while I gave up. I couldn't stay on the Internet too long. Our computer was really slow and it crashed all the time. About the only thing it was good for was writing. Before school started Dad said that we'd get a new computer for Christmas. I hoped he hadn't forgotten.

It was a miracle. We stayed inside for gym on Thursday.

Lee wasn't in school. Not that I paid all that much attention to stuff like that. Maybe I should have asked her to let me borrow that book. Or at least asked her to write down the title. It would be so cool to do a review of it. I could still hear the one line . . . *And suck the blood of all thy race.* I'd love to tell people about a book or a poem they didn't know existed.

I knew I'd make a good reviewer. Mouth probably wouldn't mind if I wrote one review sometime, but I couldn't bring myself to ask him for a favor. If I let him do something nice for me, that would make him think we were friends. Not that I could ask him right now. Mouth was absent, too. He hadn't been in school for a couple days. But that was no big surprise. All through middle school, he was out a lot. I had this image of him hooked up to a dictionary with an IV line, resupplying his word stream.

Friday, in homeroom, they handed out our report cards. It wasn't a card, actually. It was a big slip of paper. I didn't even have to get it signed. I did okay. I got mostly in the eighties. Except I got a 95 in English. Since it was an honors class, they bumped it up by 10 percent to adjust for it being a harder class. It came out to a 105, which was really beyond strange for me. I'd even managed an 85 in Spanish, which was a miracle since I still hadn't discovered the secret of communicating with Ms. de Gaulle.

At lunch, I found out that Kyle got mostly in the seventies, and a 95 in gym. He was happy. "As long as I pass," he said. I didn't show him my grades. I figured he'd give me a hard time about making the honor roll. "I've got my penultimate game tonight," I told him during lunch.

"Your what?"

"Next-to-last one. That's what *penultimate* means."

"So why don't you just say *next to last?*"

"I like the way it sounds."

"You're a total dweeb. You know that?"

"I've heard rumors. But they're unsubstantiated."

There was still no sign of Lee. Maybe she'd run off to become a poet. Or a grave digger. If that was true, the football team could have used her. They got buried that evening.

Later, while I was working on my article, I was startled by

a scream from Mom. I was halfway out of my chair before I realized it wasn't a cry of terror or pain. By the time all my internal organs had settled back where they belonged, I'd identified it as a scream of delight.

I went to the front door, where Mom had Bobby clutched in one of her death hugs.

"Hey," I said when she released him.

"Hey, squirt," he said.

I didn't get too close. He looked like he hadn't shaved in at least a week. His clothes were dirty, and he smelled like the bottom of a hamper. I think he'd hitched here. But it was good to see him.

Dad didn't give him a hard time. He just said, "Welcome home."

I could hear Bobby playing his guitar half the night. He had the volume low. I didn't mind. He plays really well. He even played in a band when he was in high school. But they all drifted apart.

I hope I don't just drift away after high school.

Bobby's return meant I was abandoned on Saturday. Mom and Dad were helping him find a cheap apartment. After I finished my homework, Kyle and I hung out at his house. I can't remember the last time we did that. I'd been so busy since school started.

"You heard from Patrick yet?" I asked.

Kyle shook his head.

"Me either."

"You won't," he said.

"Sure I will."

"No way. He's gone. Why would he bother staying in touch? It's not like we'll ever see him again."

I let it drop. I knew Kyle was wrong, but it wasn't worth arguing about.

The folks came back home about an hour after I did. "Any luck?"

"Not yet," Mom said. She got some ground beef from the fridge and started adding in all the magic ingredients that transform it into her amazing meat loaf. "There don't seem to be many places available right now. There's no rush. Bobby knows he can stay here as long as he wants. It's his home."

On Monday, Lee came up to me in homeroom and held out a book. "Here. This should give you pleasant dreams." Instead of her usual fishnet stuff, she was wearing a top with long black sleeves, but I noticed something on her wrists. At first, I thought it was cuffs from another shirt. Then I realized it was bandages. On both wrists.

"Hey, spaceboy. Take the book. Duh?" She shoved it toward my face and I grabbed it.

I could tell from the musty scent of leather that it was an old book. "I'll be careful with it." I still couldn't tear my eyes away from the bandages.

"What are you looking at?" she asked.

"Nothing."

"This?" she asked, raising her arms. "I did something stupid in the kitchen." She glared at me as if daring me to say anything more.

I thanked her again for the book, then went over to my seat.

November 19

I got this poem I've been dying to read. But I'm too creeped out to read it right now. I mean, it's not the poem that's creeping me out. Though I hope it'll be spooky. It's the person I got it from. Well, not her. But what I think she did. Okay—and her, too. A bit. Or a lot.

I'm not sure how to talk about this. The thing is, sometimes kids do bad stuff to themselves. Some kids cut themselves. Some kids even try to kill themselves.

I guess the ultimate survival tip is pretty simple: stay alive. The rest is just details. Think twice before you do anything permanent. And then think again. I don't want to say anything more about it right now. It's too creepy.

Wait. I will say something. This is too important. And if you don't listen to anything else I tell you, I hope you'll listen now. No matter what you might hear about all these tragic figures, and the whole romantic image of the suffering artist, suicide is not cool. It's not heroic. It's not romantic. It's like running away. Abandoning your family. And leaving someone else to clean up your mess. Only, it's even worse, because once you go there, you can't come back. And that would really suck.

{ seventeen }

Kyle got me in a headlock when I stepped off the bus.

"Guess what?" he said.

"What?"

"I'm wrestling."

"Obviously. Want me to wrestle back?"

"No. I mean, I'm on the team. You should try out. It's not too late." He clamped down tighter on my neck. "I'll put in a good word with the coach."

"Not a chance." Some of Bobby's friends were wrestlers, and I saw what they went through making weight. It was pretty brutal. Sweating. Starving. Spitting into a cup, for crying out loud. I mean, how much can spit weigh? And I definitely wasn't enjoying my current position as a human pretzel. Especially since it put my nose way too close to Kyle's armpit.

"Well, you should go out for some sport," Kyle said. He let go of my head and stepped back. "It's a good way to fit in."

He had a point. It was pretty obvious that you got treated better if you were on a team. Even a losing team. Except there wasn't anything I could go out for. Some kids were good at sports. Some stunk. And some were right in the middle.

That's where I was. I could shoot baskets okay when there was nobody in my face, but I was nowhere near good enough to play on a school team. Even if I grew six inches.

It would be wonderful to be good at something. I mean, I was a good reader, but that wasn't like being a good ballplayer. Actually, there was one thing I was really good at—being the youngest Hudson kid. I'd mastered the art. And now I was getting benched.

After escaping Kyle's headlock, I found myself the subject of an eyelock. Lee kept glancing over in homeroom, as if we shared some kind of secret. I felt like the guy you see in the beginning of just about every vampire movie—the first victim, who gets stalked during the opening credits. I avoided her gaze by taking out my notebook and making a list.

Seven Reasons Why Scott Hudson Shouldn't Join the Wrestling Team

1. I really have no desire to find out in person what my small intestine looks like from the inside.
2. I'd rather not have to learn to exist on a daily diet of three Saltines and a Slim Jim.
3. Most of my joints only bend in one direction—and I'd like to keep it that way.
4. I look ridiculous in tights.
5. Two things get rubbed on the mat all the time—butts and faces. This can't be good for my complexion.
6. There will without doubt be some form of painful hazing for the new guys.

7. Any activity that produces that much grunting should probably be performed in private.

When we were leaving the room, Lee waited for me by the door. "Well?"

"Well what?"

"The poem. Like it?"

"I didn't read it yet."

"You obviously have your priorities out of order." She shook her head as she spoke. I expected to hear a fair imitation of Christmas sleigh bells, but much to my surprise, this motion didn't produce any jangling from all the dangling pieces of metal.

"I guess." I slipped away. But I had the book in my backpack. So I read the poem in study hall. The title was *The Giaour.* I didn't have a clue what that meant. Didn't matter. The poem was way beyond awesome. And way longer than I'd expected. It was more than thirty pages. The part Lee quoted was the best, but there were plenty of other amazing lines. I didn't understand a lot of it. It was around two hundred years old, so some of the stuff Byron mentioned didn't mean a thing to me. Like if I wrote about my favorite TV show, people two centuries from now might not have a clue what I was talking about. But it was still an amazing poem.

November 22

Happy Thanksgiving, Smelly. I wonder whether you're currently as well developed as the average turkey? You're probably not as smart. Or as attractive.

Thanksgiving is one of the best holidays, because it's all about food. This time next year, you'll be sitting with us, eating ground-up turkey paste, or whatever it is they feed kids who don't have a whole lot of teeth. The truth is, I'm not really looking forward to watching you eat. Then again, you can't be that much messier than Aunt Zelda. With or without teeth. Maybe the two of you can share a plate. And a drop cloth.

Dad and my uncles are watching football. Before we ate, they spent a lot of time in the garage, gazing at the 'vette and making guy sounds. Mom and my aunts are sitting in the kitchen, exchanging stories about pregnancy and birth. From what I could tell, whoever experienced the greatest amount of pain for the longest period of time is the winner.

None of my cousins came. They're all older. Bobby's up in his room taking a nap. They never did find him an apartment.

Speaking of football, the last game is tomorrow. I'm glad it's over. Though I was actually starting to enjoy the games. I had sort of a ritual. I'd sit near the top so I could see everything. Not at the very top. That's where the tough guys hang out. Mouth went up there once and they dangled him over the edge and shook him until his pockets were empty.

At halftime, I'd get a cup of hot chocolate. I always drank it too soon and burned my mouth. That's another thing you need to know. Some foods are deadly. Maybe I should make a list for you.

Scott Hudson's Guide to Lethally Hot Foods

Pizza: Watch out for the cheese. It will stick to anything.
I've seen kids lose half a lip this way.

Chicken Pot Pie: The crust keeps the heat in. The sauce
is the most dangerous part. One bite can turn the roof of
your mouth into shredded flesh.

Blueberry Pancakes: The great ambusher of the food
world. Even when the pancakes seem cool, the berries
are little heat bombs. The same warning applies to
blueberry muffins.

Fried Ice Cream: The oxymoron of the food world. It's ice
cream that's coated in some kind of stuff and then
quickly fried. I know what you're thinking. How can it be
dangerous? That's what I thought, too. The first mouthful
I ever tried burned my tongue so badly I couldn't taste
anything for a week.

Hot Chocolate: Magically, no matter how long you wait,
and how much you blow on it, when you take that first
sip it's always just hot enough to scorch your mouth.

There was nothing to be thankful for on the football field that
Friday. We played South Welnerton, our traditional Thanksgiving rivals. Though *rival* might not be quite the right word,
considering they beat us 108 to 3. The scoreboard didn't even
go up that high. Maybe *executioner* would be a better choice.

I had an extra day to write my article. We always got the
Monday after Thanksgiving off. It was the first day of deer
season. I wasn't sure whether they did this so kids could hunt

or because they were afraid some nearsighted hunters would take a shot at a school bus. Either way, I was happy to have a nice quiet day to hang out, read, and eat turkey sandwiches.

Tuesday, on the way out of homeroom, I gave the book back to Lee. She'd gelled her hair into tons of tiny spikes, which made her head look like some sort of dangerous green vegetable of the sort that was always trying to kill the Mario Brothers.

"Like the poem?" she asked.

"Yeah. Thanks."

"Wasn't it cool where they—"

"I gotta go." I hurried off. I was halfway down the hall before I realized why things felt so uncomfortably familiar. This was just like in the hospital, when Tobie wanted to talk about his books and I didn't pay attention. Back then, I at least had the excuse that I wasn't much of a reader. This time, I didn't have any excuse at all. I loved spooky stuff.

I turned around, but Lee was gone.

I wished she'd never loaned me the book. When people do favors for you, life gets complicated. That's why I hadn't asked Mouth if I could write a review. But maybe Mandy would suggest it herself. There was a newspaper meeting tomorrow. With football over, I figured she'd let me do something fun.

{ eighteen }

mr. Franka had taught us to be careful about using words properly when we were writing. A phrase like *five P.M. this afternoon* is wrong because *P.M.* means *afternoon*. He gave us a whole list of stuff like that, including *free gift* and *unfortunate tragedy.* His favorite example was the sentence *The troops ran into a surprise ambush.* He pointed out that since an ambush is a surprise, the word *surprise* isn't needed.

Either way, I got ambushed on Wednesday. And it was a surprise.

"Which do you like better," Mandy asked when I walked into the meeting, "basketball or wrestling?"

That was easy. "Basketball." Of course, I liked her brown top even better.

"Good," she said, "so I'll put you down for basketball."

"What?" My jaw dropped as the meaning sank in. "Wait. That's not what I meant."

Mandy smiled at me. "Sorry. My mistake. If you'd rather cover wrestling, that's fine. You did such a great job with football, I wanted to give you first choice. You really brought an amazingly fresh approach to the task."

Book reviews! my mind shouted. That was my choice. I'd even brought a copy of *Dragonflight* with me, just to see if I could start a conversation with Mandy about fantasy series.

"So, then. Wrestling?" she asked. She leaned closer to me and smiled like she'd just offered me a sip of her soda.

I tried to think of some way to say *Neither.* I pulled my eyes from her and looked around for Mouth. But he wasn't there. He hadn't been on the bus, either. Maybe he'd be out for a long time. Then they'd have to let someone else do reviews.

Before I could speak, Mandy clapped her hands together and said, "You know what—I'm going to take a chance. Call me crazy, but I think you can handle both. That way, you don't have to decide. This is super, Scott. It'll be a lot of work, but I guess for a big sports fan like you, it's actually a lot of fun. It'll give you a great excuse to go to all the games." She glanced around the room. "Anybody else want to do any sports?"

Naturally, every other pair of eyes in the place fled from contact.

"Fabulous," Mandy said, making another note on her pad. "I'll put you down for both. That's a relief. I thought you might want to try other stuff, but this will work out perfectly." She gave me a schedule, then started handing out art assignments.

Oh, great. There were two or three basketball games a week, and one or two wrestling meets. Worst case, I'd be covering as many as five games in one week. Best case, I'd meet a vampire who'd put me out of my misery. Or a giaour.

November 28

Don't ever be afraid to ask for what you want. Nobody can read your mind. People always assume you want the same sort of things they want. I'll give you an example. Bobby likes pepper flakes on his pizza, so if I go somewhere with him, he just sprinkles flakes on the whole thing, even though that's not what I want.

So make sure to ask for what you want. Except from me, of course. And watch out for girls in tight tops. Especially when they lean toward you. Or clap. Or move at all.

"Urrrggghhhhhhhh . . ."

"Ooooooofffffff . . ."

Mr. Cravutto had found a new way to torture us.

"I miss freezing to death," I told Kyle as I tried to defeat the force of gravity by raising far more iron than anyone would ever need to lift in real life. The iron seemed equally determined to thwart my efforts.

"Weights are great," Kyle said. He got off his bench, checked out his biceps in the mirror, then peeled off his shirt and twisted at the waist so he could stare at his back.

"'Weights are great.' That was sort of a minimalist poem," I said. After that, I stopped talking and saved my breath for grunting. Mr. Cravutto filled in the silence by shouting various encouraging phrases at us and occasionally questioning our masculinity. If there's a hell, it has a weight room.

"Can't believe I survived," I said as we headed for the

shower. We'd lifted for almost the whole period. I had a funny feeling I'd be hurting pretty soon.

On the way to art class, I noticed that Lee had stuck a sign on her locker. It said *This is not a locker.* I'd hate to be her art teacher. She'd probably glue a bunch of magazine photos of people on a page, with their eyes cut out, and write something weird on top like *Art is in the eye of the beholder.*

After school, I went to a basketball game and had a completely new experience. We won. The team was pretty good.

I realized there was no way I could come up with some clever article about every single game. So that evening I wrote a short piece describing the highlights. It felt strange to just tell what happened. It also felt kind of nice. The writing didn't get in the way of the information.

Friday, when I woke up, I felt like someone had packed my muscles with ground glass.

"It'll be worse tomorrow," Kyle told me after I crawled off the bus. "Second day is always bad. Glad I've been lifting for a while."

My pain continued after school at the wrestling meet, but moved from my muscles to my mind. The team stunk. Vernon was on it. Yet one more reason for me to be careful what I wrote. In the article, when I got to his match, I just said, "Vernon Dross, at 176, fought valiantly for a minute and twenty-seven seconds." In other words, he was pinned at 1:28 of the first period.

Kyle wrestled on the JV team. I didn't have to cover that, but I went early so I could catch his match. He won. Pinned his opponent at the start of the second period. I wanted to congratulate him, but I didn't get a chance to see him afterward.

November 30

If gym grades were based on pain, I'd have an A-plus right now. Or maybe an A-plus-plus.

Congratulate me—I've managed to take on more than I can possibly handle. I'll nail my tongue to my chin before I agree to do anything else. Oh yuck—that sounds like something Lee would do. Of course, she'd use a more interesting object than a nail. An ostrich feather, perhaps. Or the shinbone of a bat.

On the bright side, I've notched off another month.

December 1

Ow. Ow. Ow. Ow. Ow. Ow. Ow. Ow. Ow. Ow. Ow. Ow. Ow. Ow. Ow. Ow. Ow. Ow. Ow. Ow. Ow. Ow. Ow. Ow. Ow. Ow. Ow. Ow. Ow. Ow. Ow. Ow. Ow. Ow. Ow. Ow. Ow. Ow.

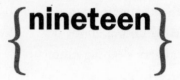

{ **nineteen** }

It was the first Monday of the month, which meant I had a student-council meeting. Since nobody paid any attention to freshmen, I sat in the back and killed time writing a fake football article. I didn't miss football, but I missed getting creative about it.

On Tuesday, I heard the following conversation in English class:

Julia: Did you see the announcement?

Kelly: Yeah. This is so exciting. Are you trying out?

Julia: Of course. I love acting. Are you?

Kelly: Absolutely. I've been in a play every year since fifth grade.

I checked the bulletin board after class. The poster was already halfway covered with other stuff, but I could see the important details. They were putting on *A Tale of Two Cities*. I guess someone had turned the book into a play. Auditions were on Thursday. Which meant I had two days to talk myself out of doing something stupid. After my experience with student council and the newspaper, I'd have to be a total idiot to try out for a play just because Julia might be in it. Not that I cared. I'd pretty much stopped thinking about her. At least, not every waking moment. Or every sleeping moment.

Besides, I didn't know the first thing about acting. Though it didn't look all that hard. I'd already given a speech. A successful speech, for that matter, that had launched my career in the exciting and glamorous world of student politics. Acting wasn't much different. Look at all the actors who ran for office. I'd bet the cast spends a lot of time hanging out together.

I'd been taking the Sheldon Murmbower shield for granted since it had been functioning perfectly for months. But Wednesday morning, he wasn't on the bus. Thanks to that, I got smacked on the head a couple of times. To make things worse, the bus was so overheated that I kept nodding off. So each slap was like some sort of medieval wake-up torture.

I saw Lee at her locker before homeroom. The sign was still there. The one that said *This is not a locker.*

Ignore it, I told myself. I started to walk past. But I couldn't help myself. Maybe the head smacks had jarred something loose. "What's that supposed to mean?" It was a stupid question. There was no reason to believe it was anything more than a meaningless slogan.

"It means nothing and everything," she said.

My response must have gone straight from my gut to my mouth, because it never passed through my brain. "That's a bunch of crap. It sounds deep, but it's just words." I could feel myself ready to start ranting. I hated it when people tossed a bunch of words at you and pretended there was some sort of deep meaning. Word were too important to be used like blobs of paint. I mean, when someone can come up with stuff as amazing as "caverns measureless to man," people have no excuse for spouting gibberish and calling it art. But I stopped dead and clamped my mouth shut when I remembered the bandages I'd seen on her wrists. I sure didn't want to be the one who pushed her into some kind of bottomless depression.

To my surprise, Lee smiled. "Just a bunch of words," she said. "That's the point. It's a meta-statement. Words about words. Get it?"

"It's still crap," I said, but without any anger in my voice.

"Ninety percent of everything is crap." She patted the sign. "And I'll bet, despite the fact that you're one of the few people in school who actually care about knowledge for its own sake, you can't tell me where that quote comes from."

I had no idea. But I wasn't going to admit that to Lee. Or stand around all day talking with her. So I took off.

When I got home, I tried to find out who said that quote. I searched for it on the Internet, but our computer was getting completely flaky.

Thursday, in English, Mr. Franka asked if anyone was auditioning for the school play. "It's a great way to get a different insight into the written word," he said. "Not to mention a chance to spend quality time with Charles Dickens."

Five kids raised their hands. Including Julia. I wasn't one of them.

That afternoon, I noticed Lee had put a new sign on her locker. It said *This is a locker.*

December 6
Auditions for the school play are tonight at seven. But I've learned my lesson. No way I'm going. I can't act. I have no interest in theater. My voice still cracks once in a while. And I'm far too busy already.

I made it to six-thirty before I asked Dad for a ride to school.

"Tell you what," he said. "I have to go to the hardware store. I'll drop you off, get what I need, then swing back and see if you're done. How's that?"

"Great."

When Dad dropped me off, kids were just starting to show up. Mine was the third name on the list. But the place filled up pretty quickly after that.

At seven, Mr. Perchal, the director, got on the stage, thanked everyone for coming, and gave the usual pep talk about trying your best and accepting that not everyone would make it.

"All right," he said. "Let's get started." He grabbed the clipboard and called the first name. Then he walked over to the piano that was sitting to the left side of the stage.

A kid, carrying a sheet of paper, walked to the middle of the stage. When the kid nodded, Mr. Perchal started playing music, and the kid started singing.

What in the world? I looked around me. Everyone had sheets of paper. I glanced to my right. It was music. By then, the second person was onstage.

"I thought we were doing *A Tale of Two Cities*," I whispered to the kid on my left.

He looked over and nodded. "Yeah, but this is the musical version. Didn't you learn a song?"

Musical? No way. This was Dickens. The French Revolution, death, and tragedy. Not song and dance. I had to get out. But I was in the middle of the row. I looked around. Ohmygod. Julia was two rows behind me, along with Kelly.

"Scott Hudson," Mr. Perchal called.

Maybe if I just stayed in my seat, he'd move on, like at the deli counter when they get to a number after the person has left.

Kelly gave me a little wave and said, "Break a leg." I should be so lucky.

I got up and walked over to the director. "I didn't learn any of the songs," I said. Maybe that would be the end of it.

"No problem." He bent over and thumbed through a pile of sheet music on the floor next to his bench. "You know 'This Land Is Your Land,' right?"

I wanted to lie. But every kid who's made it through third grade knew that song. I nodded. Mr. Perchal pointed toward the center of the stage. "Go for it."

I should have run off right then. Or pretended to have a burst appendix. Instead, I made the horrible mistake of trying to sing. I could see this shocked look on everyone's face when I let out my first note. Shock turned to horror as I produced a second note that was totally unrelated to the first. It was like they'd seen a small animal get cut in half on a table saw. My voice cracked on the third note, and never uncracked until the painful end. When I was done, Mr. Perchal didn't say a word. He just sort of nodded. I hurried off the stage.

I waited by the outside doors for Dad. I could hear the voices floating out from the auditorium. Julia sang like an angel.

"How'd it go?" Dad asked when he picked me up.

"Fine," I lied.

When I saw Mr. Perchal in the hall the next day, I ducked my head and avoided his eyes. No point reminding him of what was probably the worst experience of his theatrical career. As I started to dash past him, he said, "Got a moment?"

"Sure." I wondered whether he was going to ask me to take a vow never to sing in public again.

"How'd you like a spot on the stage crew?"

"Stage crew?"

He nodded. "Show business is more than just actors and singers."

I guess he felt sorry for me. "I'm pretty busy," I told him.

"This won't interfere with any of your activities. I promise. Our schedule is very flexible. We could really use your help. The crew is the backbone of the troupe."

"What do they do?"

"Not much. Mostly just make sure things run smoothly. The whole experience is a lot of fun. The crew and cast are like one big family. You'll see."

One big family.

It sounded perfect. I'd get to hang out with the cast and I wouldn't have to sing or dance. Or learn any lines. What could be better than that? I'd probably be able to do my homework while I sat around backstage. "Okay, sure. I'll give it a try." I could even offer to help Julia learn her lines.

"Great." He flashed me the same smile I'd gotten from Mr. Franka when he hooked me into picking the topic for April. Then, as he walked off, he whistled a tune all the way down the hall.

December 8
The folks went out to buy some furniture for the nursery. They buy stuff every week. I think you're going to have a bad impact on cash flow around here. I hope we can recover our investment when I sell you.

Who'd have thought something as simple as a crib would bring two skilled mechanics to their knees. I was smart enough not to even go into the room. Dad was kneeling on the floor, surrounded by bolts, nuts, screws, slats, dowels, and odd pieces of metal twisted into all sorts of strange shapes. Bobby was next to him, holding a screwdriver in one hand and a pair of pliers in the other. A direction sheet lay on the floor between them. Mom hovered above them, her arms crossed on her ever-expanding stomach.

"Will it be ready by May?" she asked.

Dad glanced at her, nodded, then slid the directions in front of Bobby. "Read me the first step."

Bobby pointed to the top of the sheet. "No need. There's a

diagram. Directions are stupid, anyhow. The people who write them have never put anything together in their lives."

I thought Dad would get annoyed, but he said, "I think you're right." He moved the sheet out of his way. "We won't be needing this."

Mom sighed and glanced up at the ceiling. I went downstairs. A half hour later, Mom joined me and started making a batch of cookie dough. I didn't ask her how it was going. Every five or ten minutes, I could hear Bobby shout something. Once, I heard the clatter of a tool hitting the floor.

Two hours later, when I went upstairs and peeked inside the room, they had something in front of them that Dr. Seuss might have drawn to imprison a baby Sneetch. They seemed to be taking it apart.

Sunday, when I looked in, the whole crib was assembled. There were a couple extra parts lying on the floor, but I figure they weren't important.

Monday, when I got to school, I saw a crowd of kids around the side door to the stage. I recognized some of them from the audition. I hung back, since I figured they'd probably recognize me, too. After the crowd thinned, I went over to see who'd gotten what role. I read through the list twice before the reality of it sunk in.

"I am such an idiot," I muttered as I slunk off toward homeroom.

December 10
Guess who ISN'T in the play. Take a wild guess. What's that? I can't hear you. Speak up. You're really going to

have to shout if you want your voice to get through all that amniotic fluid.

Yup. Julia didn't make the cast. Not even the chorus. I can't freakin' believe it. Neither can she, I'd bet. Especially since Kelly got a part. Julia can't be very happy about that, either. Kelly sings like a frog.

To make this whole thing even more special, I found out that the members of the stage crew have to be at every rehearsal. Worse, it's not just for a month or two. We'll start in January and rehearse all the way until April. Which I guess makes sense since this is going to be the *spring musical.* For someone who reads so many books, you'd think I'd have paid attention to those words.

You're probably laughing your head off as you read this. I guess I should remind you that right now your head is transparent, and about the size of a walnut. Or maybe a grapefruit, at best.

Rehearsals are in the evening. Later than basketball or wrestling. So Mr. Perchal told the truth—it won't interfere with any of my activities. Just with my life.

By the way—I hope you don't roll around too much in your sleep. I'm not sure your crib can take the stress.

{ twenty }

I'd gotten in the habit of looking at Lee's locker whenever I passed it. Tuesday morning, she'd put up a sign that said *This is not a cantaloupe.* But someone had written *Drop dead, freaky bitch* across it in black marker. It must have just happened. I could still smell the sweet chemical aroma of the marker. Kids passing by in the hall looked at the locker and laughed.

I stood there and stared at it when I should have been keeping an eye on the hall around me. Too late, I saw Wesley Cobble walking up. He glanced at the locker for an instant, but didn't seem to notice anything. Maybe he couldn't read. But he could see. He homed in on me and hit me up for a contribution. But after he moved on, the real problem was still right in front of me. I thought about those times on the news when they showed some symbol of hate spray-painted on a wall. Even though Lee was kind of freaky, this was just plain wrong. Someone should take down the sign. I reached out, not sure whether I wanted to get linked with her in people's minds.

I remembered Kyle chasing after the guy who'd knocked my books to the floor. He hadn't even hesitated. Or worried about getting hurt. But Kyle and I were friends. Friends stand up for each other. I tried to tell myself that this was different. I barely knew Lee. She wasn't a friend of mine. I had a hard time even looking at her face.

But it just wasn't right, no matter how I felt about her. I took the sign down and tore it up. I hoped she hadn't seen it. She might act all tough, but it had to suck when someone called you names in front of the whole school.

I watched her in homeroom, trying to guess whether she'd seen the sign. I couldn't tell.

Later, as I was walking out of English class, I heard Mr. Franka mutter, "Why do they kill us with all this paperwork?"

I wandered over to his desk. "Ninety percent of everything is crap," I said.

Without even glancing up from the piles of paper on his desk, he said, "Sturgeon's law. How true."

Score.

December 11
You know what guys do? They stand up for people. You know why? Two reasons. It's right. And it feels good. Even if the person you helped doesn't know what you did. Maybe especially then.

I wish someone would stand up for me on the bus. The head smacking continues. I've got this crazy fear that each smack drains a tiny bit of intelligence out of my head. Maybe the fact that I'm worrying about this is proof that I'm getting dumber. On the other hand, if I lose enough brain power, I'll probably stop worrying about getting smacked. Or about anything else.

What about you? Right now, you've got nothing in your brain at all. Maybe all you feel is happiness. Or a terrible, unbearable, unquenchable craving for a cheeseburger. Now, wouldn't that suck?

I think I'll go ask Mom for a grilled-cheese sandwich. Yum. All crisp and brown and buttery, with lots of tangy cheese just oozing out the sides, Mmmmmm. Yum. Sorry I can't share it with you. Enjoy your umbilical beverage.

Wednesday morning, while I was waiting for the bus and contemplating the purchase of a football helmet, Mouth started talking about his next book review.

"I'm doing *The Princess Bride* this week."

"You must have a lot of free time," I said. That was a pretty long book to finish in a week. My own life involved far fewer books than I wanted. And far more sports. My butt had been permanently marked by those rounded bolt heads that made the bleacher seats so awfully comfortable. I'd lost track of how many games I'd been to. I guess if I really wanted to know, I could count the rings on my butt.

"I didn't have a chance to read the whole thing," Mouth said. "But I rented the movie. I skimmed a lot of the book, too. I just didn't read every single word. That's one of the tricks I learned. You can get a pretty good feel for a book without reading everything. I try to pick books that are also movies. It makes reviewing a lot easier. Or short books. With those, you can read most of it. If I do a hardcover book, almost everything I need to know is already on the cover flap. Sometimes, I'll pick a book because the cover is awesome. This reviewing stuff is a lot trickier than it looks."

As if that wasn't bad enough, when I turned away from Mouth, I saw something that completely crushed my spirits. Sheldon went by. In a car. I guess his mom was driving him to school. I wanted to chase after them and scream, "Take me with you!"

When I got on the bus, I looked all around, hoping to spot a replacement decoy. I didn't see one. That's when it hit me—I was the new Sheldon.

Slightly later, I got to restore at least a pinch of those spirits. On the way out of homeroom, I caught up with Lee and said, "Sturgeon's law."

She patted me on the arm. "Well done."

I guess the head smacking really had done something to my brain, because I brought my football satire—the one I'd written during student council—to the newspaper meeting. Mandy wasn't there yet. While we were waiting, one of the artists passed around a couple really awesome cartoons he'd drawn.

"Check this out," I said. I pulled the paper from my notebook. It was too good not to share. I'd called it "A Football Feast." I compared the players to the food in the snack stand. Vernon was a hot dog, of course. The defensive line was nachos because they crumbled so easily. The offensive line was soda. They lost their fizzle early in the game. I didn't say anything bad about individual players, except for Vernon. And it's not all that bad being called a hot dog. I actually complimented a lot of the players, though in a fun way. For example, Terry Swain was pretty fast. So I said he was hot chocolate because he burned up the field, and all the girls thought he was sweet. Terry was also the center on the basketball team.

Mouth laughed so hard, I thought he was going to lose his lunch. Everyone else liked it, too. Then Mandy came in and we got down to business.

I nearly died when I got home and realized I didn't have the article. The last time I'd lost track of something I'd written, I'd ended up as a sports reporter. If this piece got in the wrong hands, I'd end up as a large bloodstain. But when I got to the bus stop the next morning, Mouth was waiting for me.

"Hey, you forgot this," he said, handing the piece back to me.

"Thanks. I can't seem to hold on to anything."

"I know what you mean." He started to tell me about all the stuff he'd misplaced.

It wasn't just papers that could get misplaced. I didn't see Kyle at lunch. Not at first. I finally spotted him over at the minor-jocks table with a bunch of the JV wrestlers. I caught up with him on the way out and asked, "What's up?" Which was really my way of asking, *What are you doing?*

He shrugged and said, "They kind of like the team to hang

out together. We're all in training, so it helps if we eat at the same table."

I waited for him to suggest that I join him tomorrow. He didn't. Maybe I should dye my hair green and start wearing black shirts with pictures of dead rock stars. And stick some pins in my face.

December 13

There's something you need to know about the cafeteria. It's a miniature map of everyone's social standing. More than any other place in the school, it defines where you belong. And where you don't belong. Imagine walking into a huge room filled with sorted students. Cool over there. Extremely cool there. Dangerous and cool that way. Dangerous and not cool this way.

I just realized there's something else you need to learn about the cafeteria. I never told you one of the most important survival skills of all.

Scott Hudson's List of Dangerous Cafeteria Foods

1. Fish in any form. (Fish sticks are safe, since they don't contain any actual fish.)
2. Turkey served more than a week after Thanksgiving.
3. Anything with *steak* in its name. Especially if it's chopped up.
4. Anything with *surprise* in its name.
5. Brown lettuce.
6. Green meat.

Scott Hudson's List of Safe Cafeteria Foods

1. Jell-O (unless the lady who sneezes a lot is working in the back).
2. Pizza (unlike real pizza, this kind is never served dangerously hot).
3. Potato chips.
4. Ice cream.
5. Fish sticks (see above).

Monday.

Hush.

It was a day of silences. In the morning, for the first time in the history of the universe, Mouth actually stopped talking. We'd just gotten off the bus and headed into the school. He was describing some of the things his dog had eaten—both organic and inorganic. Right in midsentence, he stopped. The sudden absence of sound was as jolting as the blare of an alarm clock.

A second later, I saw what had caught his attention. Lee strolled toward us, wearing a black T-shirt with two words printed on it in large red letters: FREAKY BITCH. It looked like one of those do-it-yourself iron-on things.

She grinned at me and did a very feminine curtsy, then floated on by without a word.

Mouth managed to recover his rhythm. "Oh man, they're going to send her home."

"They" acted pretty quickly. I heard her get called to the office in the middle of first period.

The second moment of silence happened to Mike Clamath at the opposite end of the school day. I saw it right after I got on the bus. Mike was leaning on Wesley Cobble's Mustang in the student lot. Wesley walked over and said something to him. Mike got off the car, but then he swung at Wesley. Wesley took the punch right on the jaw. He didn't move. Even from far off, I could see Mike's eyes change. Wesley hit him once, and Mike dropped. Then Wesley grabbed his collar and dragged him over to the side of the parking lot, out of the way of the cars. I expected Wesley to stomp him a couple times, but he got in his car and drove off like nothing had happened.

December 17
This is as good a time as any to tell you about fights. Except for complete psychos, kids really don't want to fight. Trouble usually starts for some stupid little reason. Like one kid bumps another. And the other kid says, "Watch where you're going." And the first kid, instead of just saying, "Oops, sorry," talks back. Then they both start saying stuff. All of a sudden, there's a crowd watching, and neither one can back down. So they push each other. And they're still both hoping something will happen to stop the fight. Maybe another kid will step in, but that's pretty rare. It takes a lot of guts to break up a fight when there's a whole crowd shouting for blood. So they end up fighting. It doesn't last long most of the time. As soon as one kid gets in a good shot, it's over.

But normally, the loser doesn't end up taking a nap by the side of the parking lot.

Speaking of naps, Christmas break is coming up. They don't call it that. They call it winter break. I wouldn't care if they called it the Squid Ink Interval, as long as it meant time off from school. Everyone around me looks so tired, I feel like I'm an extra in a low-budget zombie movie.

{ twenty-one }

friday, we had a half day. Finally, it was Christmas vacation. I was more than ready to kick back for a while and relax.

Usually, Kyle and I did our Christmas shopping together. When I called him, he said he didn't have time, so I went by myself. I was going to buy Dad a book about classic muscle cars, but I figured he'd like some trout spinners better. That way, he could think about fishing while we waited for spring.

I'd wanted to get Mom a cookbook, but I didn't have a clue which ones were good. And there was no way I was going to touch any sort of baby book. So I got her this nice set of flavored cooking oils. She liked stuff like that.

I bought Bobby a watch. Nothing expensive, but it kept time. I noticed he'd lost his. I also got him a couple cool neon-colored guitar picks.

December 25
"Merry Christmas," Scott said presently.
    I remember back when I was really little, Bobby and I would wake up at sunrise and dash into the living room. The presents would be there under the tree. We'd go to

Mom and Dad's bedroom, but they'd be asleep. We'd figure out some way to make enough noise so they'd get up. But I'm older now, and I can wait. I'll come back later to tell you what I got. Meanwhile, in the spirit of the holidays, here's a list especially for you.

Scott Hudson's List of Perfect Baby Gifts
A case of paper towels
Corks of various sizes
A shop vac
Shrink-wrap
Odor-Eaters

Still December 25
Well, we opened our presents. Mostly, I got some clothes. No sign of a new computer. I guess the folks are saving money for baby crap. Thanks a lot.

The vacation seemed to vanish right in front of my eyes. Before long, it was New Year's Eve. Mom and Dad were at a party across town. They were probably listening to all sorts of clever new-year/new-baby comments. Bobby was out. Probably making the rounds of a half-dozen parties. I was home, reading a book while the TV played and the end of the year approached.

At midnight, I glanced up from my book and watched the ball drop in Times Square. Right after that, the phone rang. It was Mom. I talked to her and Dad for a minute. The phone rang again a moment later.

"Happy New Year."

The voice was oddly familiar, but I was pretty sure I'd never heard it on the phone before. I tried to figure out who it was.

"Hey, spaceboy, you there? What's the matter? Vampire got your tongue?"

"Lee?" I could hear a light tapping. I realized it was the sound of a row of earrings bumping against the receiver.

"Yup."

"Uh, Happy New Year to you, too." I couldn't think of anything else to say.

Neither could she, I guess. She said good-bye and hung up. I hadn't noticed any party sounds behind her. She was at home, too. Probably alone with a book. I thought about calling her back and asking what she was reading. But that would have been pretty pathetic. I didn't want to begin the year by starting a telephone book club for people with no place to go.

January 1

I'm still pissed about the computer. But it's a holiday. In some cultures, the New Year is a time of forgiveness. Not in my culture. You're gonna pay. Somehow. Maybe I can rent you out to a lab or something. Or auction off your stem cells.

Anyhow, Happy New Year. The folks went to a party last night. It's noon and Dad still isn't up. I guess it was a good party. At least for Dad. Mom took it easy, since anything she drinks you drink, too. I don't think she wants to pickle your brain. Though if she did, I could definitely get you a job in a carnival. I heard Bobby come in around four or five in the morning. He won't wake up for a while, either.

New Year's is sort of like starting a new school. You can make all sorts of plans and promises about being better or changing your habits. Then you go on being yourself.

I guess you're lucky that way. You're really starting from scratch. Or from goo.

{ twenty-two }

It was tough going back to school. But I'd sort of missed English. When I got to class, I noticed that Julia wasn't sitting next to Kelly. They must have had some kind of fight during vacation. Probably because of the play.

On the positive side, it was definitely too cold now for even Mr. Cravutto to think about taking us outside for gym. The ground was frozen solid. But that just meant there was more time for weight lifting.

Though the first day back was reasonably easy, things got busy the next day. I had to cover a basketball game and go to play practice. When I got to the auditorium, Mr. Perchal pointed toward the back of the stage and said, "Go report to Ben. He's in charge of the crew."

I saw six guys sitting around a table, playing cards. That was good. There'd be plenty of people to share the load. I figured I'd be able to study. And maybe play some cards.

"Freshman," one of them said. He was a skinny guy with the kind of acne that looks like it's taken up permanent residence on his face. He was wearing a Phillies sweatshirt with the sleeves torn off.

The others looked over.

"Fresh meat."

"Fresh blood."

A half-dozen fresh phrases floated through the air. The guy who'd spoken first, I guess it was Ben, pointed to a stack of two-by-fours. "We need those cut into three-foot lengths."

I stared at him, wondering whether he expected me to do all the work while the rest of the crew sat and played. He stared back and shrugged.

Great. I was almost as good with a saw as I was with a wrench. Maybe they'd let me change spark plugs next.

I guess sawing uses different muscles than weight lifting, because I had a whole new set of sore muscles the next morning. But I forgot all about the pain in my arms when I came within inches of death on Friday.

Mr. Franka had sent me to the office to get a file he needed.

"I'll be with you in a couple minutes," the secretary said. So I took a seat. A moment later, Wesley Cobble came in. I thought about pretending to be asleep, but then I remembered what had happened to me when I fell asleep on the bus. I had no idea what Wesley might steal from me if he thought I wasn't conscious. Probably a kidney.

My attempt at becoming a stealth person failed. There were three empty chairs, but Wesley plopped down right next to me. I could feel his eyes on me. I really didn't want to turn my head, but I couldn't help myself.

I looked at him and nodded. Just the tiniest, insignificant gesture to show I acknowledged his presence. I was pretty sure he didn't recognize me, despite the fact that I was one of the many donors who'd contributed to his collection efforts.

That part of my plan didn't work very well, either. Instead of losing interest, he nodded back and said, "What'd you do to get here?"

I realized if I said, "I'm picking up a file for Mr. Franka," Wesley would know I was a goody-goody well-behaved kid of the sort he enjoyed pummeling. I'd end up on his radar. But I didn't want to risk a lie. So I told the truth.

"Perambulation," I said.

"Oh yeah?"

"Yeah. That's what got me here."

"Cool. I was trying to borrow a table saw from wood shop."

Phew. That was close. I'd told the truth when I'd said per-ambulation got me to the office. It was just a fancy word for walking. It definitely sounded worse. Like when people refer to chewing as *mastication*.

Wesley got called into the principal's office. As he stood up, without thinking, I said, "Have a nice day."

I flinched, expecting him to spin around and knock me out. What a lame thing to say. Especially when he was about to go see the principal.

Wesley glanced over his shoulder. "You, too, man."

A couple minutes later, the secretary handed me the file I was waiting for. By then, my pulse had dropped to a safe two or three hundred beats per minute.

I thought that was the end of my social interactions with

Wesley. Then, at lunch, who should perambulate across the cafeteria and drop down into the seat opposite me while I was masticating some macaroni and cheese? Yup. My new pal. Right in the seat that used to be Kyle's.

Wesley didn't say a word. Just chewed slowly at his roast-beef sandwich. The silence was driving me crazy. Finally, I said, "You know, Westley's the name of the good guy in *The Princess Bride*. That's pretty close to Wesley. It's an awesome book."

He stared at me for a moment, chewed another bite, then said, "Oh really?"

It dawned on me that I could get hurt just for using the word *princess* in his presence. Or *bride*. I nodded and went back to eating, though my throat had closed up so tight I could barely swallow. I could still see the way he'd decked Mike Clamath with one punch. He'd only need half a punch to flatten me.

Midway through lunch, Wesley got up and strolled out of the cafeteria. I noticed kids all over the place glancing at me as if they were trying to figure out where I fit in the social structure. Their guess was as good as mine.

January 4
My arms are going to fall off. Yesterday, I sawed a forest of wood for stage crew. Today, we moved sets all evening at rehearsal. Picture this. Seven guys are carrying a large piece of plywood painted to look like the back wall of a house, and weighing nearly as much as a real house.

Six of them are at one end. One guy is at the other.
Guess who that one guy is? If this keeps up, I'll
eventually be able to tie my shoes without bending over.

There was a student-council meeting on Monday. I had the funny feeling that if I didn't show up, nobody would notice. We spent the whole meeting figuring out what each class should sell this year for their fund-raiser. The other freshmen wanted to sell wrapping paper. I felt we should sell books.

After the meeting, I went up to the adviser and said, "Would it be okay if I quit?"

He stared at me like I was a complete stranger. "Quit what?" he asked.

"Student council."

"Oh. Right. Sure, if you want. That would be okay. What position did you have?"

"Council member."

"Freshman?"

"Yeah." I started to leave, and then turned back. "Don't you want my name so you'll know which member won't be back?"

"Nah. I'll figure it out."

On the way out, for just the slightest bit, I felt like a quitter. But then I felt like a genius. I was done with it. No more meetings. No more feeling completely ignored. It was probably the smartest move I'd made all year.

Thursday afternoon, I was standing at my locker when Julia walked by. I barely glanced at her. Hardly even noticed her dark green wool sweater, tan pants, mini–diamond-stud earrings, or the scent of peaches drifting from her freshly washed hair. Hardly noticed her at all. But a moment later, I realized Lee was staring at me like the two of us were at opposite ends of a microscope.

"Isn't that sweet," she said.

"Isn't what sweet?" I asked.

"The way your face gets all soft and your eyes get dopey whenever she's anywhere near you."

"I don't know what you're talking about," I said. Good God, Lee reminded me of Patrick. He'd figured it out right away, too. I felt like that little model of a transparent guy—the one whose skin is plastic so you can see all his organs. Especially his rapidly beating heart.

Lee's gaze skewered me. "You know exactly what I'm talking about, Romeo."

I shrugged and said, "So I notice her. So what?"

"So talk to her. She's just another person. No better or worse than you. Start a conversation. It beats drooling on your shoes."

Good grief. Lee was the last person in the world who should be giving social advice. I shook my head. "I can't talk to girls."

Sometimes, right after you speak, you can feel the universe shudder.

Lee's stare turned into a glare. "Thanks."

"That's not what I meant." But I couldn't think of any way to say what I meant without digging a deeper hole.

"It's not important," Lee said as she turned away.

I felt like such a jerk.

The next morning, I was standing at the bus stop when a Mustang drove by. The driver hit the brakes, threw the car into reverse, and pulled up to the curb. It was Wesley. Everyone in the group took at least one giant step back.

Wesley leaned over and rolled down the passenger window. "Hop in."

I figured he was talking to someone else, so I didn't move. But he looked straight at me and said it again.

I got in. He's not the sort of person you say "No, thanks" to. We shot away from the curb before I could even buckle my seat belt.

Behind us, I heard Mouth calling, "Hey, can I get a ride?"

When we reached the parking lot, Wesley hopped right out, said, "Later," and headed into the building.

Inside, I noticed that Lee had a bunch of rock stars on her locker. All the ones I recognized were dead. Underneath, she'd written *Only the young die good.*

I nodded at her in the hallway. She stared at me without nodding back. I thought about putting a picture of Beethoven on my locker. He was the most famous dead musician I could think of.

January 12

I finally figured it all out. It's too late for me, but at least I can pass this along. Don't talk. Not at all. From the day you walk into high school to the day you leave, do not utter a word. Because if you do, one way or another, you'll get some girl angry with you. There is no such thing as an innocent comment.

You might want to avoid hand gestures, too. And anything else that might carry meaning. Facial expressions. Deep breaths. Loud thoughts.

By the way, if you need any wrapping paper, let me know. I have to sell thirty rolls.

Monday morning, Wesley picked me up again. But he stopped to get coffee at the diner on Eighth Street, and have a couple cigarettes. We got to school a half hour late. And I smelled like smoke. Wesley gave me a ride home after detention. I miss getting smacked on the head. At least it's quick, and has never been linked to lung cancer.

Tuesday, I got to the bus stop as late as possible so I'd miss Wesley. There was a new kid in my seat. A big new kid. The driver started shouting, "Take a seat! You're holding us up!" I had to sit in the back. With the felons. By the time I got to school, I'd loaned all my lunch money to my seat mates. And my calculator. At least they didn't take my sneakers.

I miss riding with Wesley.

When I got the paper, there was a headline saying BIG SHAKE-UP ON STUDENT COUNCIL. Wow. I never thought I'd make the front page. I started reading the article. Fortunately, there was enough noise around me to drown out the swearword I shouted when I finished the first sentence. It seems I wasn't the only freshman who'd decided that the council wasn't a lot of fun. The president and vice president had quit. Which meant that the new freshman-class president was the person who'd gotten the next highest number of votes. Julia. Madam President.

That wasn't the only change. We had a different teacher in Spanish. Mr. Kamber. I guess Ms. de Gaulle had gone back to France. Or maybe to Madrid, to confuse the locals. I thought my worries were over until Mr. Kamber opened his mouth. His accent was so thick, it was like listening to someone speak backward. And he was chewing gum. From the few words I could understand, I was eventually able to figure out that he was from Australia.

After he'd told us about himself, he started the lesson. It went like this:

Mr. Kamber said something that might be Spanish, like *"Ramblah pasten tew eznokulacha."*

One of the kids in the class said, "I didn't understand that."

Mr. Kamber shrugged and said, *"Nwarries, might."*

And it continued.

"Tunko qweb mis decoofaloocha por abanki?"

"Huh? I don't get it."

"Nwarries, might. Echefolaka si mwarble docho."

"What? I didn't understand that."

"Nwarries, might."

After I'd heard *Nwarries, might* a half-dozen times, I finally figured out he was saying, "No worries, mate," which I guess is Australian for, "You're screwed and there's nothing anyone can do about it."

{1 7 5}

I miss Ms. de Gaulle.

Wednesday morning, I showed up early enough to catch a ride with Wesley. When he pulled away from the curb, I said, "You going straight to school?"

He grinned at me. "Want to go somewhere? I'm cool with that."

"No. That's not what I meant. I need to be on time."

He stared at me. Which made me even more nervous because he was still driving. My reluctance to lie vanished. "I've been late so much, I'm already in big trouble. One more time, and they might throw me out."

"I hear you," Wesley said. He stomped on the gas. Tires squealed. I was pushed back against the seat as the roar of eight cylinders blasted my ears and a fog of burned tire particles coated my lungs. I think I'll always be able to look back at that moment as the exact instant when I knew for sure I had no desire to be an astronaut.

"There's lots of time," I shouted, forcing the words out against the pressure of acceleration.

I doubt he heard me. He was too busy taking a turn on two wheels. Which must be even harder when you steer with one hand.

Wesley screeched to a halt in front of the school. "Sure you don't want to grab some coffee? Nothing goes on during first-period anyhow. Or second. Teachers aren't awake yet."

"Thanks, but I'd better get inside."

"Whatever." He peeled away, leaving me to wonder whether, instead of gas money, I should be offering him tire money.

{ twenty-three }

Once upon a time, well, actually it was today, I was sitting in English class.

"We can break writing up in various ways," Mr. Franka said. "Even though some things aren't meant to be broken. However, the board of education wants to make sure you all know certain concepts for testing purposes. So today we'll look at four types of prose. You'll be tested on this eventually, and probably endlessly."

I sat and listened as he explained about narrative writing. That was one of the most common kinds. It told a story.

When Mr. Franka finished that part of the lecture, he paused for a moment, sitting on the edge of the large metal desk that was wedged on a slant in the left corner of the room, beneath the drooping glory of the flag. "Who can name another type of writing?" he asked.

I raised my arm, and noticed with interest how the dust particles danced in a golden light beam coming through the window.

"Yes, Scott?" Mr. Franka said, pointing toward me with a chalk-stained finger.

"Descriptive?" I asked in a voice that was tinged with both enthusiasm and a slight shadow of uncertainty.

"Right." He nodded. "As I mentioned, it is important for you to learn these distinctions. You'll be tested on them. It might not be as much fun as reading novels, but if you don't do well on the tests, it can affect the rest of your education. So I urge you to pay attention. Now, who can name another type of prose?"

He called on Julia, who said, "Persuasive?"

"Correct." Mr. Franka then fulfilled his role as teacher, which of course required that he inform and educate us. He explained that beyond narrative, descriptive, and persuasive writing, there was another sort. Expository writing laid out facts.

"And there you have it," he said. "Though you'll never encounter all four in the same place."

First day of midterms. It was hard to believe the year was half over. There weren't a lot of kids on the bus Thursday morning. We didn't have to come in until it was time for our tests. That was third period for me, but I didn't want to hike into town, so I took the school bus. Being early wasn't a problem. I just hung out in the library and studied. I didn't even see Wesley drive past the bus stop. Maybe he skipped midterms.

The tests weren't all that bad, but I felt kind of fried. I had English, Spanish, and chemistry. Tomorrow, I'd have history, life skills, and algebra. But then there'd be a long weekend.

We had Monday off for Martin Luther King Day. No basketball games or wrestling meets during midterms, either. Naturally, I had a rehearsal scheduled for Monday morning. It was so thoughtful the way Mr. Perchal made sure practice didn't interfere with my schedule.

That night, Wayne and Charley stopped by the house. They're two of Bobby's old friends from his band. They'd been up in Boston, playing in small clubs. But the third guy in their group had been a real jerk, so they broke up. Mom invited them to stay for dinner. Afterward, I hung out with them for a bit in Bobby's room while they played music together.

"We're heading to Nashville," Wayne told Bobby.

"No more small time," Charley said. "We're going where the action is. You should come."

"I'm broke," Bobby said.

Charley sighed. "I'd spot you some money, but we're pretty broke, too. Maybe you can join us when you get some cash."

"Maybe," Bobby said.

I could see he was tempted. As for saving up some money, that was going to be kind of tough since he still hadn't found a job. Even so, he should have gone with them. It's great if you can make a living doing something you're really good at.

I told him that after they'd left.

"It's just too much of a long shot," he said. "I'd love to get the band back together, but what's the point? Besides, I'm tired of wandering around."

I could hear him pacing in his room all night.

• • •

The paper had come out on Wednesday because of the holiday. I looked through it in homeroom, even though I didn't have an article in it. That is, I thought I didn't. But there it was, on page 3—"A Football Feast," by Scott Hudson. Hot dog references and all. They'd used boldface for the players' names. And decorated the whole thing with clip-art drawings of food. Oh, my God.

This was no time to wonder how it got printed. This was the time to get as far away from the football team as possible. I got permission to go to the nurse's office. "You're pale and sweating," she said. No kidding.

The nurse called Mom, who picked me up. I talked Mom out of taking me to the doctor. I told her I just wanted to go home and go to bed. I spent the morning imagining a million variations of my death at the hands of enraged football players.

That afternoon, I called Kyle to check on things. "Did Vernon see the article?" I asked.

"Yeah. He's pissed. Big-time."

"Can you talk to him? Explain it was just a joke."

"No way," Kyle said. "I'm not getting him mad at me. One of the guys called him 'wiener boy,' and Vernon decked him."

A couple minutes later, the phone rang. It was Mouth. "Hey, Scotty, I didn't see you in school. I heard you went home sick. So maybe you don't know about this. But remember that great article you wrote? You know, the really funny one about the snacks."

"Uh-huh . . ."

"I made a photocopy for myself after the meeting. I kept

waiting for them to run it since it was so funny and everybody laughed when you showed it around at the meeting, but I guess you never turned it in to Mandy. And then there was all this space in the paper since nothing much is going on because of midterms. And you didn't have a new article. So I had a great idea. Which I guess you don't know about. Anyhow, I gave a copy to Mandy. Isn't that cool? It's too good not to share. I wish you'd seen it when it came out. It looks great. We put the players' names in bold so they could find themselves more easily. That was my idea. Don't worry. You didn't miss anything. I saved you a copy."

"Mouth," I said.

"What?"

"You're an idiot."

He laughed. "Yeah. I know. So, do you want me to drop off a copy for you, or do you think you'll be back in school soon? The last time I was out, I missed five days. Boy, the homework piles up. You think you'll be out long? Like I said, I can drop off a copy for you."

I told him I'd get a copy. I didn't bother explaining that I'd already seen it. Or that he'd doomed me.

January 23
I might get killed tomorrow. If I don't make it home alive,
you can have my books.

I managed to slink around for part of the morning without running into Vernon. But I knew I couldn't avoid him forever.

I stopped at my locker right before fourth period. Lee had stuck a note there in her distinct handwriting. All it said was *You are what you eat. So what's eating you?* I guess she'd read my article.

That's when Vernon caught up with me. Along with three of his buddies. Together, they probably had about the same mass as a small car.

"Hudson?" he asked.

I nodded. At the moment, I didn't think I was capable of producing any sort of sounds that would resemble words. At least, not out of my mouth. My butt felt like it was getting ready to issue a cry for help.

Vernon grabbed my shirt in one fist. His knuckles looked like walnuts. "You write for the school paper?"

As I nodded again, I could feel his fist tighten. At least it would be over soon. He'd punch the crap out of me—maybe all 90 percent—and in a mere five or six months I'd be as good as new, except for a couple scars, some false teeth, and an inability to remember my name or hold a conversation. On the bright side, I'd probably be able to sit through history class without fidgeting.

He curled his other hand into a fist. Behind him, his friends pulled closer. I felt like I was getting a tour of Mount Rushmore.

"Hey, Scott. What's up?"

I looked over to my right.

"Everything okay?" Wesley asked.

Instead of waiting for me to answer, he shifted his eyes

toward Vernon. I felt the grip loosen on my shirt, like Vernon had been hit by one of those blowgun darts that paralyzes all your muscles. Wesley kept staring. Vernon let go and backed up a step.

"I got that stripe painted on the car yesterday," Wesley said. He was still staring at Vernon, but talking to me. "Come see."

The bell rang for fourth period, but I didn't care. I was just happy that all of my organs were still inside my body where they belonged. I followed Wesley into the parking lot and admired the bright red racing stripe painted on the side of his Mustang. I'd never seen a more beautiful work of art.

"Very nice," I said. "It's really very . . . uh . . . straight."

He nodded.

"Thanks," I added.

"Anytime."

I realized I'd be hanging out with Wesley for a while. At least until Vernon graduated. Vernon was a senior, but with my luck and his brains, he'd be here for two or three years. Later, when I passed him in the hall, he bumped me with his shoulder. But he just kept walking. So did I.

Wesley was waiting for me after school. It actually was nice—sort of like he was looking out for me. We went cruising. Which meant we drove around without any real destination. He didn't say much. Neither did I.

There was a dance Friday night, but I had a game to cover first, and then I had play rehearsal. The cast had complained about missing the dance, so Mr. Perchal said we could leave a little early. I caught the end. Right after I walked into the gym, I remembered how little fun I'd had at the last dance. And made a note to myself to skip the next dance. I didn't even have Patrick around to help pass the time.

I had no idea why I went. Maybe I enjoyed seeing Julia with Vernon. Maybe I'd enjoy having my toenails slowly peeled away with a Swiss Army knife.

I did enjoy a fantasy. It went like this: Julia leaves Vernon in the middle of a dance and crosses the floor, coming straight to me. We dance every dance, and then walk off together, hand in hand. I spent most of the time running that scene through my mind.

Kyle was there, hanging out with the wrestlers. Mouth was there, too. He got turned down by at least seven girls in the brief time I was watching. I had to give him credit for being resilient. Nothing seemed to bother him. If I asked a girl to dance and she said no, I'd want to crawl into a hole and die.

{ twenty-four }

not all education happens in the classroom. I learned a new skill Tuesday morning on the way to school when Wesley pulled into the parking lot behind the YMCA.

"Why'd you stop?" I asked.

"Need gas." He hopped out of the car, then looked back at me and said, "Tap the horn if you see anyone coming."

"What . . . ?"

But by then he'd popped the trunk and pulled out a gas can, along with a couple feet of plastic tubing. I knew enough about the laws of physics to guess what was going to happen next.

Visions of jail danced in my head as I watched him stroll over to a car, open the door, release the gas cap, and start siphoning. Then he came back and poured the gas into his tank.

"I can give you gas money," I said when he finally slipped back behind the wheel.

Wesley shrugged. "Why?"

"So you can buy gas," I said.

"Don't need to."

I spent the rest of the trip trying to think of a counterargument. Nothing came to mind.

Wednesday, I had another near-death experience. Perry Dunlop, who's one of the seniors on the football team, cornered me on the way out of school. I figured he was going to pound me and then take his chances with Wesley.

He swung his right hand at me. I flinched. But my head stayed connected to my neck. He didn't hit me. He just gave me a friendly slap on the shoulder. Of course, his idea of a friendly slap was enough to nearly lift me off the ground.

"Your article was pretty funny, dude," he said. "Nachos. That's classic."

"Thanks." I realized Perry was on the defensive line, so he liked the joke about the offensive line. Maybe most people don't mind getting kidded, as long as they aren't being singled out.

"It's really just Vernon and a couple of his friends who want to kill you," Perry said.

"That's a relief." I felt so much better.

February 1
Another month has passed into history. Mom had some kind of ultrasound test the other day. Apparently, you have a head, hands, feet, and a working heart. And other stuff. Congratulations. You're a guy.

I woke up Monday morning to any student's favorite sound— the silence of a world blanketed by a major snowfall. No school today. I planned to hang out in my room and read. But around noon, I heard the drone of a small gas engine. Next thing I knew, a snowmobile cut across our yard. When I got to the door, I saw Wesley shouting for me to come out.

"Is that yours?" I asked. The snowmobile looked brand-new.

"Borrowed it," he said. "Get on."

I thought about the way he drove a car. But at least if we crashed the snowmobile, there'd be something soft to cushion the blow. We rode around for an hour, about half of which we spent in the air. Then he dropped me off.

"Thanks," I said.

"If the town ever floods, I can borrow a Jet Ski," he said. Then he took off.

Mom was in the kitchen, looking out the window. "You should have invited your friend in. I made cocoa. With little marshmallows."

"Maybe next time." Wesley didn't strike me as the little-marshmallow type.

Dad had gone to work. One of the mechanics had four-wheel drive.

I grabbed a shovel and started clearing the driveway. The snow was pretty light. Last year, I remember really struggling. This year, I was able to load up the shovel. Right after I started, Bobby came out and joined me.

"You heard it's a boy?" he asked.

"Yeah. You think Mom wanted a girl?"

"Nah." Bobby stuck his shovel in a snowbank. "Why would she? She already has you."

I waited until he turned his back, then nailed him in the side with a snowball.

"Ouch. Okay, maybe you don't throw like a girl."

A moment later, he whacked me with a whole shovelful of snow.

"I win," he said.

I decided a truce would be smart, so I turned my attention to the driveway.

Unfortunately, the road crews turned their attention to the streets around us, so I only got one day off.

On Tuesday, I noticed that Julia and Kelly were friends again. They acted like nothing had happened. I think girls fight differently than guys. I know I've never seen one girl knock another out in a parking lot. Maybe girls fight like brothers. No matter what happens between me and Bobby, we never stay angry for long.

When I got home, I found an e-mail from Patrick. His dad was being transferred again. He'd actually sent it a week ago, but I hadn't been online for a while. I got all excited for a second, figuring he was coming back here, or at least somewhere closer than Texas. Then I read the rest. They were moving to Japan.

That really sucked. I'd figured I could at least try to visit Patrick this summer. Texas has some of the best largemouth bass lakes in the country. I'd bet I could have talked Dad into a trip. But there's no way I'll see Patrick now.

There were more departures on Friday. Mr. Kamber left. G'day. Or, as we say in Aussie Spanish, *awdee-yowse*. Mr. Cravutto was subbing until they could find a new teacher. He didn't know any Spanish at all except some numbers. Halfway through class, we took a break to do push-ups. But we got to count in Spanish.

Lee was talking to me again. I guess she'd gotten over my stupid comment. But she looked depressed. I mean, she always looked down—it's hard not to when you dress mostly in black. But she looked really down right now.

"Something wrong?" I asked her.

"It's winter," she said.

"It's been winter for a while," I said.

"That's the problem."

"Hang in there," I told her. "It'll be over soon enough."

"But it'll come back."

I couldn't argue with that. But I hated to see her looking so down. "Hey—you need to have a little fun. You should go to the dance on Friday." As I spoke, I realized she might think I was inviting her. That would be awkward. My mind raced in search of some way to make it clear that I wasn't asking her to go with me.

But I didn't have to worry. Lee actually snorted as she walked away. I tried to imagine her dancing in the school gym, amid the paper streamers and balloons. All I could see was balloons popping when they got close to her face.

When we were driving home from school, Wesley spotted Mandy ahead of us on the sidewalk. "Mmmmm," he said. "Look at her." He slowed down as we drove past. I was afraid he was going to shout something crude. But he didn't. As much as I know he's always within an inch of doing something dangerous, I get the funny feeling he has a set of rules he lives by. It's just that they aren't any rules I ever learned.

Right before Wesley dropped me off, he asked, "What was the book with my name in it?"

It took me a second to remember what he was talking about. *"The Princess Bride,"* I told him. "Want to borrow my copy?"

He shrugged. "Sure."

I ran in and got it for him. It felt good to return the favor. I mean, he'd been giving me rides, and saving my life, and all that. Not to mention teaching me useful skills like stealing gas. After he drove off, I started to worry. It's a great book, but it's complicated. I wondered whether giving it to him was the same as showing off. I'd hate to have Wesley decide to make me eat my words. Or William Goldman's words. Page by tasty page.

To help keep my mind off that image, I tried making a list of Wesley's rules

Wesley's Rules of Life

1. It's all mine.
2. If I like you, I'll share, but it's still all mine.
3. Nothing can hurt me.
4. I can hurt you.
5. All rules are subject to change without notice.

February 13
Tomorrow is Valentine's Day. From what I see, they don't
make a big deal of it in high school. That's good,
because the whole thing with cards and flowers and all
can just drive home how pathetic your social life is.

Here's an interesting thought. I realized I can write anything I want here. I have complete freedom. Nobody is grading this. Nobody but you will ever see it. I can even write XXXXXXXXXXXX! Okay, I chickened out and crossed that off. Just in case. But it felt kind of nice to write it.

{ twenty-five }

happy artificial holiday with strong commercial overtones."
Lee handed me a wrinkled white paper bag. She was wearing
a shirt with a heart on it. I guess in honor of Valentine's Day.
Except it was a real heart.

"Happy that to you, too." I looked inside the bag and shook
it a bit. Jelly beans. All black. "I don't have anything for you."

"Reciprocity is not mandatory," she said.

"Now that would make a good T-shirt."

On the way home, I offered Wesley some jelly beans. He
shoved a handful in his mouth, took a couple chews, then
spat them out the window.

"Where'd you get these?" he asked.

"A girl I know." I flinched at the sight of his blackened
teeth.

"I hate the black ones." He spat again, then lit a cigarette. I
noticed his tongue was black, but I figured it wouldn't be
good to point that out to him. Or to laugh.

The cast convinced Mr. Perchal to let us out early on Friday,
so I got to go to the dance. It was exactly like the others. I

needed to make a note for myself. Or get a tattoo that said *No Dances*. I stood around for two hours, trying to look like I was happy to be there. I got to watch Julia dance with Vernon. He was almost as graceless off the field as on. I hope he's as scoreless, too. But there was one small bright moment. It looked like they were arguing. Julia even walked away from him for a while. I remembered Mom telling me that the smart girls got tired of the bad boys pretty quickly. But by the end of the dance, they were back together.

Kyle was with the wrestlers. A bunch of girls were hanging around with them. After a while, Kyle and Kelly started talking. I thought about how easily Mitch had walked over to that girl in the cafeteria at the start of the year. Kyle didn't look comfortable. But he and Kelly kept talking. Then they started dancing. I guess I should have felt happy for him. He'd been dying to have a girlfriend ever since Mitch got one.

Eventually, I wandered over to the snack table. Mouth was there, eating Cheez Doodles. "Aren't you going to ask anyone to dance?"

"I asked them all," he said.

"What?"

"Every single girl."

"You sure?"

"Positive. I've been keeping track. Since the first dance. I pretty much did it alphabetically. All the way through to Diane Zupstra. I ran out of girls to ask last month. I guess I could start at the beginning again, with Mary Abernathy.

Maybe that's not a bad idea. One of them could change her mind. What do you think?"

"Oh God, Mouth. I don't know. I have no idea what any girl on the planet will do. Not ever. You just can't predict how they'll act." I thought about the story "The Waltz." Even when the girl danced with the guy, he had no clue what was running through her mind.

Mouth took a sip of his soda. "You're right. There's no way to know. So it's possible someone will say yes. I hadn't thought of that. Thanks, Scott." He put down his soda and trotted across the gym.

I hadn't meant to set him up for another round of humiliation. "Wait," I called. But it was too late. He'd already gotten within range of Mary. There probably wasn't any way I could talk him out of it. I watched him get his first rejection of the evening.

There was no school on Monday. It was Presidents' Day. But we had rehearsal all morning. Given what happened to Lincoln in a theater, you'd think we'd get a break. No chance. I unloaded a ton of plywood and dozens of paint cans from a pickup truck. At least the rest of the crew joined in the painting.

On the way home, I bought this big chocolate heart at the drugstore. It was on sale cheap since Valentine's Day was over. I figured I'd wait a month or two, and then give it to Lee. I'd just have to find the right moment. Something like April Fools' Day or Roald Dahl's birthday. She'd appreciate the irony. I still felt bad about that time when I'd told her I couldn't talk to girls. Which, with a couple exceptions, was really the truth. And I felt bad about the time I'd mentioned the dance and then got worried she'd think I'd asked her.

Mouth stopped by my house late that afternoon. When I saw him on the porch, a thousand excuses raced through my mind. *You can't come in. My mom's pregnant. I have homework. It's late. My dad's taking a nap.*

But he didn't ask to come in. "Here," he said, holding out a couple dollars.

"What's that for?"

"I owe you this. Remember? For lunch."

"Oh, yeah." I'd forgotten about it.

I figured he'd spend another fifteen minutes describing the whole event, but he just said, "Thanks" and left.

Mom went on a baking spree right after dinner, making brownies from scratch. Then she made hot fudge sauce. Also from scratch. By that point, the kitchen smelled amazing. She sent Dad and me out for vanilla ice cream. On the way, I couldn't help thinking about Mouth, who'd asked every girl in sight to dance, and me, who'd never asked one.

"Did you date a lot in high school?" I asked Dad.

"No. I was kind of shy."

"You?" I knew he had to deal with a stream of people all day long at work.

"Yeah. I was the tallest kid in my class."

From my perspective, I couldn't imagine that being a problem. "Bobby's real tall. And he dated like crazy. Even back in middle school."

Dad shrugged. "I think there's more to it than height." He pulled up to the store and I ran in for the ice cream.

"You aren't shy now," I said when I got back to the car.

"I don't have a choice." He shrugged. "That's part of growing up. You do what you have to."

We brought the ice cream back home, then sat around the kitchen table and had dessert. All four of us. It was a nice way to end the long weekend. I ate three helpings. Proving that when you're young, you also do what you have to.

After Dad and Bobby had slipped out to the garage, I helped Mom stack the dishwasher. "That was great. Thanks for baking."

"It's what I love to do." She went over to the table and sat down.

"You look tired," I said.

"I just don't seem to be getting enough sleep."

"I know the feeling."

She patted her stomach. "I guess I'm sleeping for two."

"If you figure out how to sleep for three, I think I can make us both rich."

That made her smile. She reached out and put her hand on my arm. "If I could, you know I would."

"I know." We sat for a while. I could hear the sound of tools against steel in the garage. I looked at Mom's stomach and couldn't help thinking about my overstuffed backpack and all the schoolwork that lay ahead of me.

"I guess we're both carrying a lot more of a load than we're used to," I said.

"But not more than we can handle."

Tuesday I rode into the parking lot with Wesley, thinking that at least I had a short week ahead of me, and worrying about how I'd do on my algebra test. A couple minutes later, I forgot all about that stuff. I could tell something was going on because everyone was talking in little clusters.

I tapped a kid from my Spanish class on the shoulder. "What's up?"

"You know Chuck Peterson?"

"Sure," I said. Not well, but my gut twitched at the thought of bad news. "Did something happen to him?"

"No. But his mom works in the emergency room over at St. Mark's. She was just leaving when they brought in a kid from town."

"Who?"

"I don't know. All I heard was suicide."

"Oh crap. You don't know anything else?"

"Nope."

I raced to another cluster. "Anyone know who it was?"

"That weird kid," someone said. They all nodded.

That weird kid . . .

When I heard those words, I almost forgot how to breathe. Lee had been depressed all week. And she was always talking about death. I ran through the halls, trying to spot her. What if I'd given her the Valentine's present already, instead of waiting? Would it have made a difference? What if I'd actually asked her to the dance?

I raced to our homeroom, but she wasn't there, either. Or at her locker. She must have changed the sign yesterday. All I saw was a big question mark. I knew she walked here from Hamilton Street, so I ran out the front door and headed that way.

I spotted her a half block from school. I was so relieved, I could even talk when I reached her.

"Trying out for the track team?" she asked. "I'd say you run like a girl, but that's a sexist attitude."

"You're okay?" I asked.

She glanced down at her body, poked herself in the stomach a couple times, squeezed her shoulder, then looked back up at me. "Apparently. Shouldn't I be?"

"I heard some kids talking . . . something about suicide." I could hardly bring myself to say the word around her.

"You moron." She glared at me. "You really don't know me at all." Then she smiled and put her hand on my cheek. "It's sweet you were worried. Most people would probably prefer me dead. No chance—I have a zest for life. And far too many unread books."

As she took her hand away, I noticed her wrist. There was a mark there. It looked like an old burn. That day when she'd said she'd done something stupid in the kitchen—she was telling the truth.

Lee headed toward school, leaving me standing there feeling like an idiot. I also felt relieved. But she was right. I really didn't know her at all. I promised myself I'd be nicer to her from now on. And try not to say anything stupid.

I went back to the school and found out the rest of the rumor. It was Mouth. That's what they meant by "the weird kid." Nobody seemed to know for sure whether he was still alive.

It completely freaked me out that I'd seen him last night. What if I was the last person he'd talked to? I was such a complete jerk. Why hadn't I been nicer to him? I knew he talked a lot. But I could have been more patient. He wasn't a bad guy. It was obvious now that he'd been really down last night. I should have asked him if he was okay. I should have done something.

There was one small bright spot in all of this. By the end of the day, the rumors seemed to agree that he was still alive.

February 19

Hey, toe sucker. I handed in my sports article today. It's getting easier to write about the games. It's kind of like exercise, in a way. I can do more curls with heavier weights now than when gym class started. More pull-ups and push-ups, too. The first couple of times I wrote about basketball, I really had to think. Now it just rolls from my mind to my fingers.

Either way, it doesn't matter. It's just a stupid article. I need to tell you what's really on my mind. You have no idea how rotten I am. Completely stinking rotten. Nobody has a clue. Mouth tried to kill himself. When I heard about it, my first thought wasn't *I hope he's okay* or *Why would he do it?* No. You know what my first thought was? *Maybe I can do the book reviews now.* God, I'm like some kind of ghoul.

I suck.

"Is he a friend of yours?" Mom asked me at dinner.

"Not really. I know him from school."

She kept looking at me, like she wanted me to say something more.

"Mom, I'd never do anything like that. Okay?"

She patted my hand. "Okay."

I glanced at Dad. I could tell he wasn't worried.

We had a special assembly the next day. This woman talked about what to do if we felt depressed, or if we thought a friend was depressed. But what about someone like Mouth, who didn't have any friends to look out for him? At least, from the stuff they described, I was pretty sure Lee wasn't depressed. Weird, yes. Obsessed with dark stuff, yes. Depressed, no.

She'd put a couple of the dead rock stars back on her locker. I pointed to one of them. "You think it's cool, that he killed himself?" I asked.

"No. It's not cool. I think it's sad," she said. "And so infuriating. What a waste."

"Then why put up his picture?"

"Because I love his music. And I mourn for what might have been."

• • •

I covered the last wrestling meet of the season on Friday. There were regionals and stuff, but they were in Hershey, which was far enough from here that I wouldn't be going. Maybe Kyle would come back to earth now.

The last basketball game would be on Saturday. I was glad it was almost over. I could use a break. But I guess I'd just be stuck with baseball and track next.

I kept thinking about Mouth. He was probably all alone in the hospital. I tried to tell myself that he'd get lots of visitors. But I knew that was a total lie. Nobody would go to see him. He didn't have any friends. Even if he did, the whole suicide thing was incredibly hard to deal with.

Saturday, after the game, I went to the hospital. When I walked in, I got the same creepy feeling as when I'd gotten the box from Tobie's parents. That was stuff from a dead kid. This was a kid who wanted to be dead. A kid my age.

He'd tried to hang himself. Damn. I couldn't believe how easy it was to think that. *He tried to hang himself.* And how hard it was to make sense of it.

Lucky for him the ceiling fan broke. He'd lived. But he'd screwed his throat up. He had a notepad because he couldn't even talk right now. He didn't even bother to write anything much other than *Hi.* So I just babbled about stuff. But he seemed happy to see me. Which made me feel guilty. After ten or fifteen minutes, I was just too creeped out. Every time I looked at him, I thought about him dangling from the ceiling. What if he'd tied the rope to something sturdier? He'd be dead right now. I made up an excuse and split. Which added another layer of guilt to my load.

I went back on Sunday. This time, I brought him some books. He handed me a book, too, along with a note: *I was going to review this. Can you?*

For a minute, I couldn't talk, either. Or breathe. Or swallow. I felt like such a bastard. "I'll try," I said.

He moved his lips. No sound came out, but I could tell he was saying, "Thanks."

I looked at the book, expecting another Bucky Wingerton adventure, but it wasn't anything like that. It was a new collection of short stories about vampires. Some of my favorite authors were in it.

I read the whole book that night, but I couldn't bring myself to write a review even though I was dying to tell people about it. I'd feel like a vulture if I did that.

By Monday, the jokes had started. It was always like that. No matter how bad something was, sooner or later people started making jokes. Sick jokes. I heard all sorts of versions of how Mouth just wanted to hang out or hang around. A real swinging dude. All choked up. None of it was funny.

Just as I was about to walk into my art class, Danny Roholm grabbed my arm and said, "I know why Mouth did it. He wanted to get away from hearing himself talk." He started to laugh.

Something inside me exploded. I shot out my hands and slammed Danny against a locker. It happened so fast, I didn't even know I was doing it. He looked like he was going to take a swing at me, but I stared him down. There must have been something in my eyes. My face felt like it was washed in flames. After he slunk off, I realized I was shaking. I'd never done anything like that before.

Damn. Where'd that come from? It was like something Wesley would do. Except if he'd done the pushing, Danny wouldn't have been able to walk away. Maybe you are who you hang out with.

At the newspaper meeting, after talking about how awful we all felt, Mandy said, "Who wants to handle book reviews until Louden gets back?"

A couple hands shot up. I kept mine down. Mandy looked right at me anyhow. I shook my head.

"You sure?" she asked.

I nodded.

"I guess we'll shift you to baseball and track, Scott," she said. "Okay?"

"Fine." That was probably just what I deserved.

Yet more sports appeared in my life. I went bowling on Thursday. Not by choice. I was riding home with Wesley when he got on Route 22 and took it over to the Hadley exit. We pulled into the lot at Melville Lanes.

I didn't protest, since it wouldn't do any good. And since we were doing something legal. Well, mostly legal. Wesley managed to get a couple sodas from one of the machines without paying. I'm not sure how.

On the way home, he said, "Did you know the kid who tried to off himself?"

"Sorta," I said. *Please don't make a joke.* If he said something stupid, I'd probably do something even more stupid. I really wasn't in the mood to get tossed out of a speeding vehicle. Though maybe, out of courtesy, he'd pull over and beat me up on the sidewalk.

But Wesley just shook his head and said, "Bad stuff."

"Yeah."

"If I die young, it won't be by choice." He laughed and shook his head. "At least, not by my choice."

{ twenty-six }

Scott Hudson settled back in his seat and opened his note-book. As always, he glanced briefly to the side, two rows to his left, where Julia sat. As always, he sighed. Up front, his teacher began a lesson.

"We're going to learn about viewpoints today," Mr. Franka said.

Cool, Scott thought. He enjoyed the way his teacher was able to take a story apart without killing it. Mr. Franka was definitely a surgeon and not an assassin.

"In third-person limited," Mr. Franka said, "we see the world of the story through the eyes, ears, and mind of just one character. We only know what he thinks and observes."

Scott was already familiar enough with the concept. He thought about some of the books he'd read that used this viewpoint.

"In omniscient voice," Mr. Franka said, "we can flit from person to person." He scanned the rows of students, pleased to see that they were paying attention. It was a good honors class this year. "But some readers find that the omniscient viewpoint doesn't allow them to develop a bond with the characters. At times, if handled poorly, it can even be jolting."

I'm hungry, Kelly thought.

Mr. Franka discussed other variations of the third-person viewpoint. Then he said, "A few books use second person. But this is tough, and can be a bit of a gimmick."

Sometimes, the writer could suck you right into the character so well that you were almost unaware of the viewpoint. You open the book and start reading. You feel like you're actually in the story. You go right along with it. Though you probably agree that viewpoint can be used as a gimmick.

"And then there's first person," he said. "One of the characters tells the story."

I listened as he talked about viewpoint for the rest of the period. It was all pretty interesting. I'd found that with some really good books, I had a hard time remembering what viewpoint they used.

As I was leaving class, Mr. Franka waved me up to his desk. "I'll need your decision before the end of the month. How about you let me know by the twenty-fifth?"

"Sure," I said. "No problem." As I spoke those words, my mind searched for any clue to what he was talking about. I desperately needed a dose of omniscience, but his thoughts remained his own. Maybe if I could get him to talk some more, I'd get a hint. "You sure you don't need it earlier?"

"No. That will give me plenty of time to gather the materials."

"Yeah. I guess." Still no real clue. "So, the twenty-fifth? Sure. I'll make a note." I hovered there, hoping he'd say something else.

When he didn't, I headed for the door. I was almost out of the room when he said, "Scott?"

"Yeah?"

He pointed to the wall above the blackboard. I saw a poster that said APRIL IS NATIONAL POETRY MONTH. I'd completely forgotten that I was supposed to come up with our topic for that month.

"You didn't forget, did you?" he asked.

"Of course not."

Thank goodness he wasn't omniscient either.

March 3

It's quiet. Bobby's out somewhere. Mom and Dad went for a drive in the 'vette, which is actually almost running. Dad's put a ton of work into it. So has Bobby. Mom could hardly squeeze in the passenger seat. It was like watching someone stuff a roll of socks into a paper-towel tube.

My mind's been stuck on the weirdest thing. The other day, I almost got in a fight with Danny. I'm glad I didn't. Not because I'm afraid. But I was thinking. He's already really unpopular. What if he got so upset about losing a fight that he tried to kill himself? It would be my fault.

I should go visit Mouth again.

The school finally found a new Spanish teacher. Ms. Phong seemed very nice. She smiled a lot. We communicated with gestures since she didn't appear to understand English.

Even so, I was happy to see her because I was getting tired

of doing calisthenics in class and hearing Mr. Cravutto shout, "Suck it up, *bambinos*."

Nobody had the guts to tell him that *bambinos* wasn't Spanish.

I went to the town library after school and spent a couple hours trying to figure out what we should study in English next month. We'd already covered everything I could think of.

On the way home, I stopped at the corner store to look at magazines. As I browsed through the rack of comic books, I got a great idea, but I figured there was no way Mr. Franka would go for it.

I didn't get back to see Mouth until the end of the week. He'd finally healed enough to talk.

"Hi," he said when I walked in.

That's the shortest sentence you've ever uttered, I thought. Damn. Look at me. I was still making jokes. I truly sucked.

He didn't talk much. His voice was kind of raspy. Maybe it hurt. Or maybe he was all talked out. I wanted to ask him *Why?* Instead, I said, "You feeling okay?"

He shrugged. "I guess."

I waited for him to say more. But he just lay there, looking kind of spacey. Maybe they had him on some kind of drugs. But I had to know. "Why'd you do it?" I asked.

"Why not . . . ?"

"Because you can't," I said. "It's cheating, Mouth. That's what it is. Cutting in line. Or cutting out of line. You can't do that. You've got to stick with it." I stopped. In my ears, my voice was starting to take on the meaningless drone of Mr.

Cravutto when he urged us to dig deep and stick it out for another lap. *Come on, babies, suck it up. Hang in there. Pump those legs, you gutless losers. Keep it going.*

"Nobody likes me," Mouth said.

I didn't bother replying with the obvious lie. *Oh, don't say that—you've got tons of friends.* "Nobody likes me, either," I said. "I cope."

He shook his head. "Lots of people like you."

"Right. Sure." I wasn't there to argue with him. But he knew as well as I did that if I threw a party for all my friends, we could fit in a phone booth and still have room for pony rides and a moon bounce. Mitch was little more than a memory. Patrick was in Texas, and on his way to Japan. Kyle spent all his time with the wrestlers, even though the season was over. I hoped we were still friends, but I didn't really know. According to the numbering system, I was presently a member of the Zero Musketeers.

I dropped down into the chair next to Mouth's bed. "Let's face it—with a few exceptions, nobody likes anybody."

He nodded.

That was a grim statement. And I didn't really believe it. I mean, I hoped that deep in my heart I didn't believe it. Half the time, I didn't know what I believed. But at least this got Mouth thinking about how his loneliness, or whatever it was that drove him too far, wasn't unique. We all suffered. And I guess we all had good times, too. Man—if every person who ever felt lonely killed himself, the world would be littered with corpses. And far lonelier.

When I was getting up to leave, I finally asked him the question that had been haunting me. "You remember the dance?"

Mouth nodded.

"You weren't going to ask any girls to dance. But I talked you into it." I paused, trying to find the right words. "Did that have anything to do with . . . what happened . . . ?"

He shook his head. "No way. You were being nice. Nobody else in the whole school cared at all."

"So I didn't make you do anything?"

"I made myself do it," he said.

I nodded and headed out of the room. When I reached the hallway, Mouth called after me, "Scottie."

"What?"

"Cheer up."

"I'll try."

Even if Mouth said it wasn't my fault, I still felt that everyone in the school shared the blame. All of us had done our part to crush him. Monday morning, when I got in the car with Wesley, I decided to speak up.

"You shouldn't take people's lunch money," I told him.

"Why not?"

"Well, how'd you like it if someone took your money?"

He laughed. "Fat chance."

"Imagine if you weren't very strong?"

He frowned for a couple seconds, then shook his head. "I can't imagine that."

I searched for some way to get him to understand. "You have any little brothers?"

"Nope."

"What if you had a little brother? Think how he'd feel if someone took his money."

"I'd kick the guy's butt."

"Sure you would, after you found out. But think how your little brother would feel while it was happening."

He was quiet for the rest of the ride. But when we pulled into the parking lot, he said, "I guess it would kind of suck."

"It would definitely suck."

I hoped this was a sign that the school had just become a bit less stressful for the small and the weak.

By then, the jokes had pretty much stopped. It was like nearly everyone had forgotten about Mouth. Or like he'd never even existed. In a way, as far as Zenger High was concerned, I guess he'd succeeded in dying.

I wondered how small a ripple I'd leave if I vanished.

A couple days later, I got a letter from him. He thanked me for being such a good friend, which made me feel really rotten. He wouldn't be coming back. His parents were sending him to a different school.

When I told Lee about the letter, she said I should feel good that Mouth took the trouble to write to me.

"But I never liked him," I said.

"It doesn't matter," she said. "You were nice to him. At least, nicer than most of the kids. Right?"

"I guess."

"So what's harder, being nice to someone you like or being nice to someone you don't like?"

I saw what she meant, but it didn't make me feel any better.

March 15

I just got back from the dance. I think they purposely space them just far enough apart so I always forget how little fun it is to stand around drinking soda and eating potato chips while other people pair up and flail at the air.

Other than that, I had a great time.

It was a St. Patrick's Day dance, though that holiday actually falls on a Sunday this year. If you've been paying attention, you'll spot a discrepancy. (And also a vocabulary word.) Notice anything that doesn't fit? Here's a hint. Think about Christmas and Easter. I'll tell you the answer in a day or two.

In the meantime, here's a list for you.

Things That Happen So Far Apart That You Forget How Bad They Are

School dances

Dentist appointments

Hernia tests

Award shows

Chicken goulash in the cafeteria

• • •

I spent another week looking for ideas for English class. Still no luck. The deadline had arrived. I went up to see Mr. Franka at his desk before class.

"So, whatcha got, Scott? Something hot?" He flashed a grin to let me know he was aware of the painful way he'd phrased the question.

Two words popped out of the vacuum created by my panic. "Comic books." I backed up a step, expecting a lecture on taking things seriously.

Mr. Franka glanced over at the cabinets where he kept the books. "Good choice."

"Really?"

He nodded. "At least I won't have to scrounge around and dig up materials. I was afraid you'd pick something like advertising slogans or bumper stickers."

"You'd let us study stuff like that?"

"If it's written in English, we can study it. Even knock-knock jokes are worth studying. Not to mention shaggy-dog stories. But I like your choice. Besides, we'll be doing slogans for a day or two next month."

I wandered back to my desk. On the way, I thought up a dozen other things I could have suggested. But I was happy we were doing comics.

The center on the basketball team, Terry, said hi to me in the hall when he went by. He probably had me mixed up with someone else. But maybe I looked familiar to him since I'd gone to almost all the games last season. I'd never received a nod from so far above my head.

Some of the baseball players had started saying hi to me, too. I wondered whether it was because I'd written about how well the team was doing. Even better, this girl on the track team smiled at me. I was actually having fun with the articles. Not like before, where I did all that crazy stuff for football. That was fun, too, though in a different way. Back then, I was trying as hard as I could to avoid writing a sports story. Now I was trying to write the best sports story possible.

Last week, I'd written about how the other team couldn't seem to get warmed up. When I was doing my rewrite, I changed it to: *Their engine was running but it kept sputtering, like a lawn mower tackling the first grass of the season.* Maybe that was a bit much, but I felt pretty good about it.

As fun as it all was, I was looking forward to a break. Wednesday was a half day. After that, no school for a week. No games to cover, either. There were only three things I wanted to do—sleep, nap, and doze.

In other news, Ms. Phong was gone. *Ahhhdyos nguchachos.* Mr. Cravutto was back. We took two breaks for push-ups.

March 31
Happy Easter. When you're old enough to walk, I'll go outside and hide eggs for you to find in pathetically obvious places. Easter is by far the best holiday for chocolate. Halloween is probably second. They have little else in common.

It's also spring break. College kids make a big deal out of the whole thing. They go to Mexico or Florida and party for a solid week. You can see it all on MTV. But you know what—I have this sinking feeling that it's just like the dances. If I went to Cancún, I'd be standing in a corner watching other kids have fun. Though I guess instead of potato chips, I'd be eating tortilla chips.

Wow—I just realized how pathetic that sounds. I don't want you to think I feel sorry for myself all the time or that I don't expect to ever have any fun. Things are okay.

Well, mostly okay. Did I mention we have rehearsal every evening during vacation? Half the time, the rest of the crew sits around while I drag the sets all over the place. Show business sucks.

Speaking of Easter, did you figure out what's weird about the St. Patrick's Day dance? Here's the thing. They can't have a Christmas or Easter event, but they can have one named after a saint. Actually two, if you include Valentine's Day. As for what all of this means, I'm clueless.

{ twenty-seven }

thanks to Scott, we'll be studying comic books this month."
Mr. Franka's announcement was greeted with cheers. Then he
said, "But first, we're going to read *about* comic books. So
we're going to start out with a marvelous volume called
Understanding Comics."

As he walked over to the cabinet where he kept textbooks,
I could feel the mood change in the room. I knew everyone
was glaring at me. It could have gotten ugly. But the book Mr.
Franka passed out was written like a comic itself. How cool
was that? I survived the class without being beaten to death by
an angry mob hurling some boring textbook at me.

Naturally, my escape from death was balanced the next day
by a foolhardy plunge toward destruction. I was cruising with
Wesley after school. All of a sudden he swore and pulled to
the curb. There were three guys on the sidewalk, hanging out
by the mini-mart on Dwyer Street.

"They've been ducking me for weeks," Wesley said. He
hopped out of the car and walked toward them. "Pay up."

The guy in the middle said, "What if we don't feel like it?"

"You want to find out?"

I had no idea what this was all about—other than money. I don't know why they owed him. All I knew was I couldn't sit there. It was three against one. So I got out of the car and joined Wesley. Now it was three against one and a half. Actually, I knew one other thing. I knew I was terrified.

The three guys barely glanced at me. But the guy in the middle dug into his pocket and pulled out a couple twenties, which he handed to Wesley.

We went back to the car. I went back to breathing.

"You didn't have to do that," Wesley said.

I just nodded. I wasn't sure I could talk without squeaking.

"Thanks," he added. He drove two blocks, then pulled into the lot of another mini-mart. "They have great cocoa here. With little marshmallows. I love those little marshmallows."

April 8

I stood up with Wesley today. Side by side. Shoulder to shoulder. Okay—make that shoulder to elbow. Not that he needed me. Still, it felt good. I wish I'd stood up for Mouth when everyone was trashing him. At least I stood up for Lee when that note was on her locker.

Sorry to get all serious, but it's been on my mind. I mean, Kyle stood up for me all the time, but then he just dropped me for some new friends. I don't get it.

Or maybe I get some of it. Kyle needs to be part of a group. So when our group started to fall apart, Kyle found a new one.

Here's something a bit more positive—I think I just

wrote my best article ever. It's about a girls' track meet. I didn't use any gimmicks or clever stuff. I just found the perfect words, and the perfect mood, to describe what happened. Listen—here's my favorite part:

When Erica Mason cleared the first hurdle, it seemed as if she didn't believe in gravity. By the end of her race, the cheering crowd had joined her in joyous disbelief. The rarefied air of magic continued into the high jump, where Kate Bayler soared to a new personal best, skimming the bar with breathtaking elegance.

Not bad, huh?

No more calisthenics in Spanish class. When we came in on Monday, the new teacher had already written her name on the board. Ms. Cabrini. I didn't have my hopes up.

"Hello, class," she said to us in perfect English. "I'm looking forward to teaching you."

That got my attention. So did the next thing she said. "I was born in Argentina. I've also lived in Spain and Mexico. I've visited Puerto Rico and most of the countries in Central America. There are many dialects of Spanish. But, with a bit of practice, you'll be able to make yourself understood all over the world."

She picked up the textbook. "We may as well take up where your last teacher left off." Then she started reading the lesson.

I stared at her, completely lost. It sounded wonderful. It sounded like Spanish. I just didn't have a clue what any of it meant. Without hearing it in a French or Australian or Vietnamese accent, I couldn't understand a word.

Caramba.

Tuesday, I walked up behind Lee in the hall with a copy of the paper and tapped her on the shoulder. Even though she didn't like sports, I figured she'd enjoy my article. She turned and gave me this odd smile with her lips closed. Then, just when I was about to say something clever about how she should broaden her reading interests, she opened her mouth, curled her lips, and hissed. But it wasn't the hiss that spooked me. It was the fangs. She had vampire teeth.

There's nothing like an unexpected encounter with a set of overgrown canines to drive home the true meaning of fear.

"Will you cut that out?" I said after I'd regained the ability to speak and determined that my pants were still dry.

She spat the teeth into her palm. "Cool, huh?" Then she held her hand out. "Want to try them?"

"Ick. No way."

She rubbed them on her shirt. "You sure?"

"Positive."

She popped them back in. "Thuit yourthelf." She gave me another hiss, then danced down the hall, leaving me with the paper in my hand.

When I got home, I showed the article to Mom. "That's really wonderful," she said after she'd read it.

That night, I held out the paper to Bobby. "This is my best article yet," I told him.

"Cool. Put it on the bed. I'll read it later," he said.

He didn't look busy, but I didn't argue with him.

April 10

Three different girls checked me out when I walked down the hall in school today. They must have read my writing and decided they wanted to get to know me better. I think that by the end of the year, I'll have a fan club. Girls think writers are awesome.

Guess what we're learning about in English class? The unreliable narrator. That's what you call it when the person telling a story isn't telling the truth. Like in what I just wrote. Unfortunately.

And sometimes, the narrator is lying to himself. Maybe that's what I'm doing when I remember how well I knew Julia back in kindergarten. But I don't think so. I really believe we were sort of friends once.

The point is, you aren't always going to be told the truth. It's funny. I listen to different people different ways. When Mr. Franka tells me something, I just assume it's right. Even though he's always telling us to examine and question everything we hear.

When Lee tells me something, I figure there are twenty layers of meaning hidden in her words. Or maybe no meanings at all. I still haven't figured it out. With Wesley, on the other hand, he says exactly what he means.

Patrick was always pretty honest. So was Mitch. With Kyle, I used to assume that half the stuff he said was bull, but it didn't matter. You take your friends for what they are.

When Mom and Dad tell me something, I don't even think about whether it's right or wrong. I just know it's the law. It's the same, I guess, with Bobby. You get used to listening to your older brother and doing what he says. Hey. That should work out fine for me, shouldn't it, slave? I mean, brother.

Mr. Franka has this huge file cabinet full of comics and graphic novels. We could read any of them that we wanted, as long as we wrote up a response afterward. I even wrote one of my responses as a comic. I knew it was sort of an obvious thing to do, but Mr. Franka liked it and gave me a 98.

There were some pretty cool old horror comics in the piles, and these weird modern ones that didn't make a whole lot of sense, but were still sort of fun to read. I think they were the graphic equivalent of modern poetry. Someone was scamming someone. But that's okay. The art in them was pretty amazing. And some of the old comics didn't make all that much sense, either.

I figured I'd buy a couple of the really cool ones at the magazine place in town and send them to Mouth.

On the way home from school, I finally asked Wesley if he'd finished *The Princess Bride*. He'd had the book for ages.

"Yeah."

"Did you like it?"

"Sure."

"So you're done with it?" I asked.

He nodded. "Gave it to my cousin."

"Oh." At least he'd liked it.

"Got another good book?" he asked when he pulled up at the house.

"Tons," I said, though in my mind I saw my shelves slowly growing empty as the contents of my library shifted, book by book, to Wesley's cousin.

After dinner, when I walked past Bobby's room, I noticed the school paper on the floor. Bobby was sitting on his bed listening to music.

"You read it?" I asked.

He nodded. "Nice job, little brother."

"Which part did you like the best?"

"Hard to say. It was all real good."

Oh man. I knew those lines. I knew that whole routine. "You didn't read it."

Bobby shrugged. "Not yet."

"Come on. It's not that long." I really wanted him to see what I'd done. Especially since it was my best article.

"I said later."

I picked up the paper and held it out to him. "I'll wait. Come on—it'll only take you five minutes."

"Not right now."

"Come on." I jabbed him with the paper. "Just read it."

Bobby ripped the paper from my hand and threw it across the room. "I said later!"

"You jerk." I stormed out of his room. Who cared if he read my article. Who cared if he read anything.

April 15

It's tax day. Dad always gets weird around now. He almost never gets angry. But this is one of the few times of the year when the wrong thing can make him yell. Mom keeps telling him he should go to one of those tax places, but Dad insists on doing the taxes himself. He'll spend all evening surrounded by hundreds of pieces of paper. That's not his natural environment, and it makes him edgy. On the bright side, trout season opens this Saturday, which more than makes up for the tax stuff.

{ twenty-eight }

We got our report cards on Friday. I didn't care. I had something else on my mind. I kept thinking about how I'd never seen Bobby with a book. I couldn't even remember him ever looking at the newspaper.

After school, I grabbed *Tuck Everlasting* from my bookshelf, then went to track Bobby down. He was in the garage, fiddling around beneath the hood of the 'vette.

"Read this," I said, holding out the book.

"Do I look like I have time to play around? I have to get this idle adjusted."

"Not the whole book. Just the first page. Here."

He smacked the book out of my hand. "I'm busy. What is it with you? You keep bugging me to read stuff. Go get a hobby or something."

I bent down and picked it up. "Just the first paragraph."

He smacked it again. "You're being a real pain."

I picked it up. "One sentence."

"Scott, knock it off. Stop fooling around. I've got stuff to do. Maybe if you didn't waste so much time with your nose in a book, you wouldn't be such a creepy little loser."

I felt like I'd been punched in the gut. *The hell with you.* I backed up a step, clutching the book so hard I could feel the cover ripple.

No. That's what he wanted. To drive me off. Bobby knew exactly what he was doing. But I wasn't going to play that game. I waited a moment, until I was sure I could speak, then said, "I'm not fooling. I'm dead serious." I held the book out again, wondering if he was going to hit me.

Instead, he grabbed the book and opened it. As he read out loud, my heart ripped wider and wider. It was a struggle. Each word. Each syllable. After an eternity, he finished the first paragraph.

He shoved the book at me. "You happy now? I'm stupid. Okay. Is that what you wanted to know? Does that make you feel good? You're smart and I'm stupid." He threw the wrench, hard, against the engine.

I ducked as it bounced back out, but stood my ground. "How'd it happen?" I asked.

"I don't know. It's just always been hard. The words don't make sense."

"But your teachers. . . . ?"

"I learned that if I caused enough trouble, nobody would notice anything else. They never figured out how stupid I am."

"You're not stupid. You were smart enough to fool everyone. And it's never too late to learn." I thought about how hard it must have been for him to sit through year after year of school while all those kids around him could read. "Oh man, Mom and Dad don't know, either."

Bobby shook his head. "That's been the worst part."

"They'd understand."

"Don't you dare tell them anything."

I held up a hand. "I won't. I promise. But you should."

"I can't." Bobby ducked his head back under the hood. "I hope the baby isn't like me, Scott."

"I hope he's a lot like you," I said.

April 19
Listen, just because you're younger doesn't mean
you can't give me advice. Once in a while. For really
important stuff. But not all the time. So, if there's ever
something you absolutely need me to know, tell me. I'll
listen. I might hit you afterward, but I'll definitely listen.

Opening day. It was the only time I didn't mind getting up early on a Saturday. Dad was already in the kitchen making a pot of coffee when I came down.

"Want some?" he asked.

"Sure." It wasn't bad once I added enough sugar.

Bobby joined us a couple minutes later. He nodded at me like nothing had happened. I played along. Fishing is like having a truce with the world. When you're out on the stream, you leave the crap of the world behind.

We headed to the McMichaels, up in the Poconos. It wasn't as crowded as the Bushkill or the other streams near us in the valley.

Standing there, I felt for the first time in ages that there were some things that weren't changing. At least not changing so fast I felt dizzy.

A minute or two after we started, Dad hooked his first fish. By ten, he'd caught his limit. I caught three brook trout. Bobby just caught two, but one of them was a nineteen-inch rainbow.

"Keep it?" Dad asked as Bobby cupped the rainbow in his hands.

"Nah, we have enough." Bobby released his fish back into the stream.

I let mine go, too. We had plenty for dinner with just Dad's stringer. When we got home, he cooked them. Plain and simple. Right in the frying pan with a bit of butter. It's one of the few times he cooks, except when he's grilling.

April 20
We're going to do a lot of fishing. You and me. You, me, Bobby, and Dad. I wonder whether Julia likes to fish. Some girls don't, because of the worms and stuff. But she doesn't seem like the squeamish type. I'd bet a girl can be really gorgeous and still like cool things.

Speaking of gross stuff, guess what? I saw you kick. Mom showed me. No offense, but it was pretty freaky. All I could think of was science-fiction movies. Mom has an alien life-form in her gut. But you definitely know how to kick. I think you might be the first soccer star in the family. The school football team could use a kicker, too.

And a quarterback. And a wide receiver. And pretty much everything else.

Athlete or not, I'm going to make sure you learn to read.

"We taking the 'vette?"

"You bet."

Thus Dad and I composed our own couplet. It was Take Your Child to Work Day. Also known as Get Out of School for Free Day. We zoomed, sputtered, and lurched our way to the dealership. Dad stuck to the back roads since it would be pretty inconvenient to break down on the highway at rush hour.

I wasn't allowed in the garage, where the mechanics do the actual work, so I had to hang out in the front office, where Dad deals with the customers. But it was nice spending time with him. He has to wear a button-down shirt, but he refuses to wear a tie.

People came in almost nonstop, dropping their cars off for service and asking questions. They wanted to know all sorts of stuff.

"I drove a hundred miles with that oil light flashing. Do you think I hurt my engine?"

"What's the best type of soap to wash my car with?"

"Is it bad when smoke comes out from under the hood?"

"I hear this weird thump every time I hit my brakes. Is there something wrong with them?"

Dad answered the brakes question by popping open the trunk and taking out a two-liter bottle of soda.

At one point, this old man and woman brought their car

in for an oil change. I was looking through the large window into the garage, watching a guy putting a car on a lift, so I wasn't paying a lot of attention, but I heard the man ask if the job could be done today. They didn't have an appointment. The woman explained that they were going on vacation tomorrow.

"I'm sorry," Dad said. He sounded puzzled. "I don't understand."

That was weird. I looked across the service counter at the couple.

"Please," the man said. "Can you?"

"What?" Dad asked. He glanced over at me.

I knew an oil change didn't take long. Assuming I wasn't the one doing it. In that case, it would take about half a lifetime. I turned to Dad. "Can you fit them in for an oil change today? They're going on vacation tomorrow."

"Sure," Dad said. "No problem. We'll have them all set in half an hour."

"No problemo," I told them. *"Media hora."* And then my jaw dropped.

Caramba!

"Gracias," the man said, thanking me.

"De nada." Oh, my God. I'd been speaking Spanish. I'd understood them—at least, enough of the words to know what they'd been asking—and answered them. Ms. Cabrini had done it. She'd made a Spanish speaker out of me.

"Thanks," Dad said after he'd taken care of them.

"No problemo."

. . .

I actually had a complete break that day. The play started tomorrow. There was no rehearsal the night before. That's a theater tradition, I guess. We'd already had our dress rehearsal, and I'd survived it without getting crushed by any of the scenery we'd moved in the dark. But I was beginning to understand why everyone kept saying, "Break a leg."

I got two free tickets for the play, since I was on the stage crew. I thought about giving them to Mom and Dad, but Mom hadn't been going out a whole lot. And Dad didn't like to sit and watch stuff. He won't even see a movie unless it's under two hours. I gave one ticket to Lee. "You'll like it," I told her. "People die." I left the other ticket on Bobby's bed.

And, inspired by going to my dad's workplace, I finally asked Lee what her folks did.

"My mom's a phlebotomist."

I guess she figured she'd stump me. But I was up to the challenge. "She draws blood, right."

Lee nodded.

I thought about Lee's fondness for vampires. "You must be very proud of her."

"For sure."

"What about your dad?"

She made a face. "My dad's a complete failure."

"Wow. Sorry." I hadn't expected that. "He can't get a job?"

She shook her head. "No. He has a job. He's a lawyer. He was the smartest guy in his class, and you know what he does? He spends his life helping companies get around antipollution laws." She sighed. "Any way you look at it, I am the offspring of bloodsuckers."

April 25

You'll be real proud of Dad when you see him at work.
He's in charge of the whole repair department. All the
mechanics come to him when there's a problem. I hadn't
been there in years. I forgot how busy the place is. They've
got fifteen lifts. There's a constant stream of cars coming
in for repairs. He hardly gets any break all day.

If you're good with your hands, like Dad is, it's a great
job. The funny thing is that since he's so good, he
doesn't get to work on the cars. He has to spend his time
managing the place. Like if some guy isn't happy with
how his car was fixed, Dad has to deal with it. I know
he'd rather be up to his elbows in grease. That's probably
why he spends so much time at home working on the
'vette. I have a funny feeling that if he was fixing it as a
job, he'd have been done a long time ago. But since he's
doing it for fun, he's taking his time.

Anyhow, you'd have been real proud of him. I was
proud of him, too. I didn't tell him or anything. Guys don't
do that. Though, when I do something great, you can feel
free to make an exception.

{ twenty-nine }

Now the fatal blade was startin'
To descend toward Sydney Carton
But he was taking heart in
Knowing that Darnay did get away.
Darnay
he
got
awaaaaaaaaaaaaaaaayyyyyyyyyyyyyyyyyyyyyyyyyyy!!!!!!!

I pulled the curtain closed as the last note of the final number faded, then opened it for the curtain call. I'd been too busy running around and carrying props to see much of the play. But I heard it all. When the audience clapped at the end, I pretended the applause was for me.

We had five more performances scheduled between that weekend and next. Then it would be over. That was fine with me. Show business wasn't anywhere near as much fun as people thought.

Julia was there, waiting for Kelly. I watched them walk off together. It was nice that the play hadn't ruined their friendship, though I was still sort of bummed it hadn't started a new one between Julia and me. Wesley was there, too, sitting right up in the front, all the way to the left of the stage. When I thanked him for coming, he shrugged and said, "No problem. It's way easier than the movies."

"To understand?"

He looked at me like I was an idiot. "To sneak in."

Over on the right, far up the aisle, I saw Lee heading toward me. "I'll catch you later," I said to Wesley.

As he turned to leave, I headed over to cut Lee off. I had the feeling they shouldn't be allowed to get too close to each other. It would be like a snake and a mongoose.

"Great job," she said. "You really managed to minimize the thumps and crashes."

"Of course. I'm a trained professional."

She glanced past me toward the stage. "I love that guillotine. Can I have it when you're done? It would look so great in my room."

"I'll ask Mr. Perchal."

"Tell him I have a ton of stuffed animals that need drastic body modification, and this would make the process so much easier."

"That's definitely a compelling argument."

I checked with him right after Lee left, though I didn't pass along the details of her request. He said it was school property and he couldn't just give it away. Score one for the stuffed animals.

• • •

As thrilling as it was to be part of the exciting world of the theater, I took greater pleasure in my journalistic efforts. I was sitting on my bed Tuesday evening, leafing through the school paper, when Bobby came in. He held up the play ticket. "Hey. Thanks for this. Did I miss it?"

"Nah. It's on again this weekend."

"Any good?"

"Not bad. For high school."

He glanced down at the paper. "You write another one?"

"Yeah. Want to—" I stopped before I could make a jerk out of myself by asking if he wanted to read it. Then I thought about sitting in the kitchen with Mom, reading to her from *To Kill a Mockingbird*. I picked up the paper. "Want to hear it?"

"That would be great."

I read the article to him. I was a little nervous at first, but then I sort of enjoyed reading it out loud. It was nice hearing my words spoken—even if I was the one doing the speaking. I caught a sentence or two that I wished I'd rewritten, but most of it sounded pretty decent.

"That's good, Scott. Really good. You have a gift."

I shrugged. "It's nothing."

"Don't ever say that. It's very good. Honest."

"Thanks."

Bobby paused by the door on his way out. "I haven't been much of a big brother . . ."

"Are you kidding? You've been great. You take me places. You teach me all kinds of stuff about cars and music. And you saved my butt lots of times. Remember when those big kids were chasing me?'

"They were little," he said.

"Maybe to you." It was back when I was in first grade. Bobby had saved me from a group of third graders. When he was around, nobody ever picked on me.

He smiled. "Man, they sure took off when I showed up." The smile faded. "Scott . . ."

"What?"

"You're not really creepy. I shouldn't have said that."

I help up the paper. "And you're not stupid. This isn't your fault. Someone should have realized you needed help."

"Someone did."

I wanted to say it was no big deal. But my throat had gotten kind of tight, so I just shrugged.

As Bobby turned away, he said, "I'm lucky you're my brother." He went back to his room before I could tell him I felt the same way.

In a couple minutes, I heard an old song drift through the walls. He was playing "While My Guitar Gently Weeps."

April 30

Don't get your hopes up, but I'm thinking that maybe it won't be all that unbearable having another brother. At least for the brief period you're around here before I find a buyer.

I start my penultimate month of school tomorrow. I love that word. Here's something for you to think about. *Penultimate* means *second from last*. What do you think they call the thing that's third from last?

• • •

"Okay," Mr. Franka said, "you cruised along for a month reading comics. Now it's time for some serious contemporary literature."

I groaned along with everyone else, but I figured whatever he handed out would be interesting. We'd read some really difficult stuff scattered throughout the year, but none of it was boring.

A minute later, I was staring down at a script on my desk. Not a play, either. This was a movie script, for *Terminator 2*.

"Welcome to Hollywood," Mr. Franka said.

That weekend, we gave the last two performances of the play. When the crew was striking the set—in other words, when I was clearing the stage and the other guys were horsing around—I spotted Bobby standing in the back of the auditorium. I hopped off the stage and walked over to him.

"Not bad," he said.

"You liked the play?"

"Nah. But the stage crew rocked."

"Thanks."

"This whole school thing—you're doing good. Way better than I ever did. I think you can do whatever you want. Anything at all."

"Except find the right wrench."

Bobby shrugged. "There are plenty of guys who can do that. I'm serious—except for that wrench thing, I'd bet you could do whatever you set your mind to."

"So can you," I said.

"No way. I'm just good at one thing. And right now, nobody's buying. There are a zillion guitar players out there. Hey—you want a ride home?"

"No thanks. Believe it or not, I have a social event to attend."

I finished up with the props, and then went to the cast party. It was sort of like the dance. I stood around drinking soda, eating potato chips, and watching everyone else mingle. At least Julia and Vernon weren't there. *You can do whatever you want.* If only that were true.

Kelly was there. What I wanted to do was walk over to her and ask if she'd ever heard Julia mention me. But I didn't have the guts. I did overhear her say, "They've been fighting a whole bunch." I couldn't tell who she meant, but I had my hopes.

Mr. Perchal came over and clamped his hand on my shoulder. "Well done. I hope we can count on your help next year, Scott."

I mumbled something about needing to make sure it would fit in with my other activities. I had a feeling my career behind the curtains had gone as far as it was ever going to go. Between rehearsal and performances, I must have carried a grand total of about 87,000 tons of lumber. On the other hand, next year I could sit back, play poker, and let some poor freshman do all the work. The thought of that made me grin.

Toward the end of the party, Ben came over, punched me on the shoulder, and said, "Good job, frosh." That was sort of nice, but after each of the other guys on the crew repeated the praise-and-punch routine, I was hurting. But it was a good sort of hurt.

And then there are bad hurts.

They taught us on the newspaper that every story had to answer the questions *who, what, when, where, why,* and *how?* On Monday, coming out of the locker room after gym (which is the *when* and *where*), I had an unanticipated *what* with a totally unexpected *who.*

Say what?

Say this: I got in a fight with Kyle.

I'd decided it was time to test Bobby's belief that I could do anything I wanted. This seemed like a good place to start. And I was willing to take the risk that Kyle would kid me about it. We'd just reached the door when I said to him, "Hey, maybe you can get Kelly to mention me to Julia, and see what she says about me."

"Forget it," Kyle said. "She's out of your league."

Ouch. Kyle was my friend. At least he had been until he became a jock. Friends weren't supposed to be brutal about stuff like that. "You're not exactly in Kelly's league," I said. "Or anyone else's. She probably wouldn't even look at you if you weren't a wrestler."

He pushed my shoulder. "Yeah, well who's standing around all by himself at the dances?"

"Like you weren't?" I pushed him back.

"Not anymore." He pushed me with both hands.

I held off from pushing him back. I didn't want this to get out of control. "I could get a date if I wanted," I lied.

"With who? Some freaky bitch with a face full of pins?"

The air in the hallway suddenly felt ten degrees warmer. Those words were way too familiar. "What did you say?"

Kyle's eyes shifted away for an instant, then locked back on mine. "Freaky bitch."

"You're the one who wrote on her locker."

I expected him to deny it. Instead, he shrugged. "Hey, it looks like you're not the only creative writer around here."

And there went the *why*.

I tackled him. No pushing. No working up to it. I just dove at him like a madman. Which should have been a big mistake. Everyone knows it's a bad idea to tackle a wrestler. That's the first rule of fighting. If a guy knows how to fight on the ground, you have to stay away and use your fists. If he knows how to box, then you try to wrestle him.

The second I grabbed Kyle, I realized I was in trouble. He'd just finished a whole season of wrestling. He'd have no trouble destroying me. A couple seconds later, when I pinned him down, I was as surprised as anyone. So the *how* has to go unexplained.

Kyle started swearing and saying he'd kill me. I let go, stood up, and stepped back, still not really believing I'd handled him so easily.

That's when Mr. Cravutto broke things up. It figures. Gym teachers never stop a fight until they see it's pretty much over.

Kyle glared at me when he walked off. I guess I'd known for a while that we weren't friends anymore, even though I didn't want to believe it. Until that moment, I'd still sort of hoped things would go back to the way they'd been. But here's the reality of things. Kyle was once my second-best friend. Bobby was once my flawless hero. Julia was once my kindergarten pal. And I was once my parents' youngest son.

Unlike cars, lives don't have a way to go in reverse.

May 9

I got in a fight with Kyle. The weird thing is, he should have kicked my butt. I've been thinking about it for the last two days. The old me never would have beaten Kyle. But between gym class, stage crew, and calisthenics in Spanish, I guess I put on a bit of muscle.

It's funny. In my mind, I'm this skinny kid who usually doesn't lift anything heavier than a book. But my shirts are getting kind of tight across the chest. And my pants are short. Normally, Mom would have been on my case to get new clothes, but she's pretty distracted right now with this swelling sibling of mine (yeah, you) who's prevented her from seeing her feet for the last couple months. I haven't gotten any clothes since Christmas.

Now that I think of it, last week when we were doing fitness tests in gym, Mr. Cravutto actually said, "Nice hustle, Hudson. Way to go." Once you get to know him, he's not such a bad guy.

All the stuff I said before about getting out of gym—don't pay attention to that. Okay? It's good to work out. You and I can lift weights together when you get older.

Maybe you'll actually have the sort of big brother who can protect you. I think we'd both like that.

{ thirty }

the hallway walls were filled with posters on Friday. Gallons of tempera paint had been sacrificed to spread the word that there was a dance next week. It was the final dance of the year, so some kids made a big deal out of it.

As I stood near one of the posters, reminding myself that I hated dances, Julia and Kelly walked by. Right after they went past me, Kelly glanced back over her shoulder, smiled, and winked. I had no idea what that meant. Maybe it was her way of saying hi to someone who'd been part of the play. Or maybe an insect had just flown into her eye. Either way, I soon had something more important to deal with. Instead of a bug in the eye, it was more like a foot in the mouth.

Lee had taken one of the smaller posters and stuck it on my locker. Underneath, she wrote *Let's go*. For an instant, I thought she was serious. Then I realized it was typical Lee humor. Another weird locker message with layers of meaning.

When I saw her on the way out of homeroom, I said, "Good one."

"Good what?"

"Your joke about the dance."

There was just the slightest flicker across her face, like she'd almost burned her fingertips. The expression vanished so quickly, it could have been my imagination. But in my gut, I knew it was real. If I'd said something immediately, I think it would have been okay. But I could hear Kyle's words: *some freaky bitch with a face full of pins.* My brain slowed to a crawl, lost in a search for the right words.

"Yeah, it was a good one, wasn't it." Lee headed off, leaving me there with a dozen replies jammed in my throat.

I was such a jerk. I guess she thought it would be fun to go to the dance together. And I'd acted like the idea was a joke. Which meant I'd acted like she was a joke. I couldn't even imagine how much that could hurt.

I'd lied to Tobie in the hospital. I'd never stood up for Mouth. I couldn't take a third strike. I had to make things right. But I didn't know how. *I'm sorry* wasn't good enough. Not even close. Those were just words. Half the time people said them, they were lying.

Mr. Franka had some words for us. "I know we have another month of school, but I need to tell you this now. You are one of the finest classes I've had the privilege to meet. There's a lot of talent in this room."

It was nice to get praise from a teacher I really liked. But I wondered about his timing. I raised my hand.

"Yes, Scott?"

"You aren't quitting or getting sick or something, are you?" *Or dying?* I left that unspoken.

He laughed and shook his head. "Not at all. Just feeling

grateful. I was talking with a friend last night who's having a lot less fun with his students. In truth, his classes are a total nightmare. So I really felt the need to tell you what a pleasure it's been." He looked around the room, then said, "Okay, don't get misty on me, or I'll make you all read something truly gloomy where the wonderful teacher dies, along with parents, friends, and assorted pets. Now let's get back to the lesson."

I glanced over at Kelly. She winked again, but when I whispered, "What?" she just whispered back, "You'll see." After that, I couldn't catch her eye again.

I figured I could talk to her in the hall, but at the end of the class, as I was walking out, Mr. Franka put his hand on my shoulder and said, "I mean it."

I turned back toward him. "Thanks. You're a good teacher. You've showed me stuff I didn't know about."

"That's my job." He pointed to his desk, where two coffee mugs sat, each filled with pencils. One was for the Marines, the other for Lafayette College. "I took a winding path, but I'm glad I ended up where I am. The main thing is, use your gifts. And enjoy the trip."

I couldn't help laughing.

"What's so funny?" he asked.

"Now you're starting to sound like someone in one of those books."

"Right. The kindly, wise teacher sharing his wisdom with his favorite student. Sorry." He gave a fake snarl and said, "Get out of here, you little monster."

• • •

The good feeling stayed with me through the rest of my classes. At the end of the day, I felt another hand on my shoulder as I was leaving my locker. Hoping it was Lee, and that all was forgiven, I turned around and found myself face-to-face with Kelly.

"What's going on?" I asked.

She gave me a weird smile. "Your secret's out. Someone wants to see you about the dance," she said.

My breath caught in my throat for a moment. I finally managed to say, "Who?"

"You'll see. Come on." She turned and walked down the hall.

I tried to calm myself. I didn't want to start babbling. Kelly led me to the multipurpose room at the far end of the corridor. "In there," she said, giving me another wink.

This time, my voice wouldn't break when I said hi. I took a deep breath, opened the door, and went inside. I scanned the seats. She wasn't there.

I noticed some motion out of the corner of my eye. As I started to turn, something hit the back of my head. I was caught completely off-balance. As pain exploded through my head, I tumbled to the floor, landing in the aisle between the seats.

A jumble of explanations ran through my brain. I'd walked into something. A piece of the ceiling had fallen. I started to push myself back to my feet when I was hit by a stream of swearwords and knocked back down by a kick to my side.

I knew the voice. Vernon.

Another kick rocked me as I curled up.

Other words rained down among the swearwords. "You like her? Huh?" Another kick. "Well, you stay away from her."

I was hurting all over. Dizzy. He grabbed me. Lifted me to my feet. "She's mine. Don't you dare even look at her again."

Another punch. Knocking me across a row of seats. I didn't try to get up. I braced for more, but I guess he was satisfied. I heard the door open. I waited for the sound of his footsteps as he left. Instead, I heard another voice.

"You hurt him!" It was Kelly.

Then a third voice joined in. "I thought you were just going to shake him up a bit," Kyle said.

"I shook him up, all right. It felt really good."

"He needs help," Kelly said.

"He'll be fine," Vernon said. "I hardly touched him."

"Yeah. He's got a hard head. It's all stuffed with words. Let's go," Kyle said.

I was afraid to find out how much damage Vernon had done. I just lay for a while, sprawled across the seats. Finally, I took a deep breath. My ribs hurt, but I didn't think anything was broken. I felt the back of my head. There was a small lump there. My left eye was starting to swell shut and my cheek hurt.

I pushed myself to my feet and staggered out of the room. The halls were empty. Wesley was waiting by his car in the parking lot.

"You all right?" A slight frown crossed his face.

"Yeah."

"We have business to take care of?"

I thought about Wesley kicking the crap out of Vernon. As satisfying as that would be, I could imagine things growing from there until someone really got hurt. "No. It's over."

"You sure?"

"I'm sure."

"Frozen peas."

"What?"

"Frozen peas. Put them on your eye when you get home."

Mom let out an assortment of gasps when I came in. I guess my face looked a bit roughed up. "What happened?"

"Softball. A grounder hit a rock."

"Sit down." She pushed me into a chair, then grabbed a pack of frozen peas from the freezer. Apparently, Mom and Wesley had some common knowledge. "Here. Hold this on it. I don't know why they play those dangerous sports in school."

After the initial shock of the cold, it felt good. Mom hovered over me. "I'm fine. Really."

When I gave Dad the softball story that evening, he said, "Did the ball have a name?"

"Yeah. But it's not important."

"Fair fight?"

"Not really."

He reached out, put his hand on my chin, turned my head slightly, and stared at my cheek. "That's not too bad. Probably be sore for a couple days. Any other damage?"

"Nothing permanent."

"Is it over?"

"Yeah."

"Need me to do anything?"

"Nah. I'm okay."

"All right. But if you find yourself heading for any more trouble, tell somebody. Okay?"

"Look, you don't have to worry. It's really over."

He nodded and let it drop.

Bobby didn't come home until after dinner. When he saw me, he slapped me on the back and said, "All right. The squirt's not just a lover, he's a fighter."

May 10

Watch your back. It's a rough world out here. But if you do get hurt, there's one good thing. That's when you find out who really cares about you.

Hey—maybe that's not the only good thing. I feel a list coming on.

Scott Hudson's List of Good Things About Getting Beaten Up

1. You don't have to wait until nighttime to enjoy the stars.

2. It's a great way to make sure your blood clots properly.

3. Bruises break up the monotony of an ordinary complexion.

4. It's sort of fun to think about how much his fist must hurt.

5. It's nice to know there really is a use for frozen peas.

Speaking of fights, I just finished reading *The Man in the Iron Mask*. It could just as well have been the ironic mask. The book is another story about the Three Musketeers. You know—one for all and all for one. But in this story, they break up. I'd always figured they stayed together forever.

I had no trouble sleeping late. My eye didn't look too bad when I got up Saturday afternoon. I guess the frozen peas had helped. But my ribs ached. The bump on the back of my head was a lot smaller, but still sore. As much as it sucked to have gotten jumped, and as much as I felt like a total idiot for believing that Julia was waiting for me in the multipurpose room, there was something else that felt even worse.

I asked Bobby, "You ever hurt a girl's feelings?"

He shrugged. "Couple times. Never meant to, but it happens."

"So, what did you do about it?"

"Nothing I could do. They get over it. Or they don't."

I thought about stealing the guillotine for Lee. But, as much as I was picking up a lot from Wesley, I couldn't bring myself to do something I knew was wrong. Besides, if I gave the guillotine to her, I didn't think the first head she severed would belong to a stuffed animal.

That evening, I went out to the garage and asked Dad, "Did Mom ever get really angry with you?"

"Once or twice."

"What'd you do to make up?"

He pointed to the radiator cap. "What's the first rule?"

"Don't take the cap off while the water's hot."

Dad nodded.

"So you waited for her to cool down?"

"Yup."

"But what if she didn't?"

"If your mom was the sort of person who stayed mad forever, we'd never have stayed together in the first place." He tilted his head toward the workbench. "Fetch me the three-eighths box wrench."

I got it right on the second try.

May 12

It's Mother's Day. I might as well teach you the basics now. This is the day we pamper Mom. That means she gets breakfast in bed. After she eats, we give Mom her presents. Later, we take her out to dinner. But she didn't want to go this year.

"I'm as big as a house," she said.

That's an exaggeration. But not all that much. You're not exactly a compact model. On top of that, Mom's due pretty soon.

Dad was way ahead of her. Around six, this limo pulled up in front. How's that for slick? You can learn a lot about life if you pay attention to the things Dad does.

"Let's go," he said.

"Forget it," Mom said. "I'm not going out in public."
But from the way she was staring out the window at the
limo, I could tell she wanted to be talked into it.

"Trust me," Dad said. When he says that, Mom usually
listens.

We got in the limo and went on a luxury tour of all the
best fast food in town. We drove along from place to
place, munching tacos, burgers, shrimp, and french fries,
and drinking sparkling apple cider. Mom ate just a little
bite at each place. Dad and Bobby and I pigged out. Then
we got dessert. And I got an idea.

Kelly, Kyle, Vernon. Who else? Did other kids know what
happened? It sucked enough to get beaten up. It would be
worse if everyone knew. Vernon would probably brag to his
friends, like it was some kind of great achievement to jump
someone who was half your size. When she'd seen what happened, Kelly had seemed shocked. As for Kyle, I just didn't
know.

As I walked through the halls Monday morning, I looked
for any sign that the word had spread. One of Vernon's pals
grinned at me. But other than that, I didn't get any sense that
I was a news story. Fine with me. I'd just as soon forget the
whole thing. When I walked past Kyle, he avoided my eyes.

I expected Lee to avoid me, too. But she looked straight at
me and tried to act like the whole dance thing was a misunderstanding. I could feel a coldness behind her words. The

worst part was, I'd never seen her hide her feelings or pretend about anything. This must have really cut her deeply.

In English, the moment I sat down, Kelly glanced over and whispered, "I'm sorry."

"Forget it. You didn't know." I glanced past her at Julia, wondering how much Kelly had told her. Probably everything. That's what girls did. They told each other everything. I could just hear them.

Scott Hudson has this major crush on you.

Who?

Scott. You know. Sits next to me in English.

Him? That runt? Are you kidding?

No. Really. As if he had a chance.

Julia must have thought I was a total loser. And I guess she was pretty much right. I'd spent a whole year hung up on a girl who would never be interested in me. And treated the one girl who wanted to go to the dance with me like she didn't matter at all.

Maybe it wasn't too late. I had to keep trying. When I got home from school, I called Wesco Limos. They were the only local place listed in the phone book. I figured if I went way overboard—limo, flowers, and all that stuff—she'd have to agree to go.

"Everything's taken this weekend," the guy on the phone said, "except for one luxury stretch model."

"How much is that?" I asked. Nothing wrong with a bit of luxury.

"Seventy-five dollars," he said.

I wondered whether he could hear me gulp. That was kind of steep, but I wouldn't need it for the whole day. Just to pick up Lee, drop us off at the dance, and then come back later to take us home. "How much for a couple of hours?" I asked.

There was a pause. Then the guy said, "Look, kid, it's seventy-five an hour. Six-hour minimum."

"Oh . . ."

"I take it you aren't interested?"

"I guess not."

Tuesday, when I tried to talk to Lee, she said, "You know what I keep thinking about?"

"What?"

"I remember you telling me about how you were nice to Mouth even though you didn't like him. And now you're being nice to me. Is it my imagination, or is there a pattern here?"

"This is different," I said.

"Those are just words, Scott."

Words were all I had. I needed to figure out some way to make things right. I couldn't let her think I was just being nice.

I tried again the next day.

"We're going to the dance," I told her.

"I wouldn't be caught dead there," she said. "Actually, I guess if I were dead I wouldn't really care where I was. I'd just never be caught alive there. Especially not with some guy who's constantly worried about what other people think." She stepped close to me—right in my face. "Better run. People might see you talking to me."

I had to fight to keep from glancing around to see who was watching us, but I stood my ground. This close, I could see individual bits of black flakes in her eye makeup. But I took it as a good sign that she was talking about death. "Look, I'm going to be at your house at seven on Friday. I'll wait out there all night if I have to. But I'll be there."

"Whatever makes you happy. Better bring a tent."

"Seven," I said. "I'm looking forward to it." Then, as she started to move away, I reached into my backpack and pulled out the heart-shaped box of Valentine candy that I'd been saving.

"What's that?" she asked.

"It's not a locker." I held it toward her. "And it's not a Valentine." *But maybe it's a peace offering.*

She shook her head and walked away. But she took the candy with her.

Dance or no dance, I still had a mountain of assignments to deal with. I was in my room after school, trying to get stuff done when I heard these weird sounds.

"Heee, heee, hooo, hooo."

I went downstairs. Mom and Dad were in the living room. Mom was lying on the floor. Dad was sitting next to her with a checklist.

"You okay?"

"We're fine," Mom said. "Just practicing my breathing."

"Natural childbirth," Dad said.

"Right." I went upstairs, got my books, and headed for the town library. I really didn't want to be around them while they ran a dress rehearsal.

I stayed at the library until I figured it was safe to go home. I was halfway there when a car skidded to a stop by the curb right in front of me. Vernon's car. It was my turn to make strange sounds.

I expected a gang of his friends to pour out and rip me to pieces. Instead, Julia scrambled out and slammed the door.

"You jerk!" she shouted.

Vernon yelled back, but the words were drowned out by the sound of screeching tires as he shot away in a cloud of blue smoke.

I didn't know which of us was more in shock. Julia looked stunned. She seemed like she was trying to figure out where she was. As she turned my way, I guess I was the first thing she recognized.

"Scott . . ."

"You okay?" I asked. I was halfway surprised she remembered my name.

She nodded. Her body jerked a couple times as she bit back a sob.

I took a step closer. "Did he . . . hurt you?"

She shook her head. "It wasn't anything like that. He wouldn't hurt me. It's just—we fight. He gets angry. I get angry. It's been real bad the last couple days."

"I'll walk you home."

"Thanks."

She was quiet until we were about a block from her house. Then she sighed and said, "Why does everything have to be so hard?"

I didn't have an answer for her. The silence returned as we covered the last block. Couldn't she see that she was way too good for Vernon? I thought about how I hadn't realized I'd changed. Maybe Julia hadn't realized how much she'd changed, either. I wondered what images hovered in her mirror. An invisible girl?

"You're so lucky," she said when we reached her house.

I had no idea what she meant. I waited for her to explain. Instead, she said, "Kelly told me you'd asked about me."

All I could manage was a nod.

She glanced away for a moment, then looked right in my eyes. "I guess you probably have a date for the dance . . ."

The words were right there if I wanted them. *No, I don't have a date.* It would be so easy. And it wasn't really a lie. I didn't have a date. Lee had turned me down. To my credit, only a couple seconds passed before I opened my mouth and killed a thousand fantasies with a single sentence. "I've asked someone."

"My loss." She put a hand on my shoulder and kissed my cheek, right where Vernon had hit me. Then she went inside.

Damn.

May 16
Here's a big tip for you. No, make that a HUGE tip. Never assume anything. For example, don't go around thinking a girl doesn't like you unless you have indisputable proof.

I guess that leads to a second tip. If you like a girl, tell her. Because you have no way of knowing what she's assuming, either.

Hey, I'll bet you thought I forgot about the word for *third from last*. Did you make a guess? It's *antepenultimate.* How's that for cool? I guess it might be a real handy word for you to learn, since you're the third-from-best kid in the family.

{ thirty-one }

the phone woke me late that night. Someone picked it up after the second ring. I drifted back to sleep, but then I heard another sound.

Guitar music. Real quiet. I couldn't even make out the song. I got out of bed and went to Bobby's room.

"What's up?"

"You know Charley?"

"Sure. The guy from your band." A ripple ran through my gut. Late-night calls meant bad news. "Is he okay?"

"Yeah." He shook his head. "It's like a million-to-one shot. He met this girl down there. She's a secretary for a concert promoter. The opening act for this tour broke up. They need a new band right away. Charley managed to talk the guy into giving him an audition."

"Good for him," I said.

"It's still just the two of them down there. He wants me to join them."

"Great. When's the audition?"

"Tomorrow afternoon."

"In Nashville?"

Bobby nodded.

"So go," I said.

"No way to get there."

"Take the 'vette."

He shook his head. "The clutch needs work. And she's been burning oil. The distributor is still messed up, thanks to me. I screwed it up pretty badly with the wrench. I'd never make it even halfway there."

"Take Mom's car. Get down there, do the audition, catch some sleep at Charley's place, and come back the next day. What is it—a ten- or twelve-hour drive?"

"Yeah. Think they'd mind?"

We both glanced toward their bedroom. I was sure Bobby was thinking the same thing I was. *Wake them and ask permission?* Bobby looked back at me. We both knew the basic rule—when in doubt, don't ask. I also knew Bobby was trying hard to act more responsibly. It was up to me to give him a push.

"They'd be thrilled," I said. "Dad can take the 'vette to work, right? Does it run well enough for that?"

"Sure. It might smoke a little, but it should be fine for a short hop as long as he doesn't push it too hard. And he loves driving it."

"Then do it. He won't mind. He's proud of you."

Bobby looked at me like he wanted to say something more. "Go," I said.

I stood by his bedroom window and watched him drive off. I was glad he had the courage to take a chance. Maybe it would work out great. Maybe not. But at least he wouldn't spend the rest of his life wondering what might have been.

Later, as I was trying to get back to sleep, I realized Bobby hadn't only driven off in search of his dreams, he'd also driven off with my ride to the dance. The 'vette was a two-seater.

"Nashville?" Mom said when I told her the news the next morning. "Please tell me this is a joke."

"It's no joke." I decided not to add that it was my idea.

Dad stared toward the garage for a minute. "Did he have enough money for gas?"

"Yeah. I gave him some."

Mom and Dad exchanged glances, and had some sort of silent conversation. I expected them to be angry. And I think they were, at first. But then Mom said, "Bobby's been chasing something all his life. Maybe this is it."

"It's a long shot," Dad said.

"But what's the harm?" Mom said. "Whatever happens, I'm glad he went. You've got your dream. Someday you'll have your own garage." She looked at me. "I want my boys to follow their dreams, wherever they lead. Even if I don't always understand them."

"He'll be back tomorrow," I said. I wanted to tell them more, to help them understand why Bobby had gotten into so much trouble. But that was his decision. I headed off to school, to chase after my own small goal.

I tested the waters when I saw Lee in the hallway by saying, "Hi."

"Hi." No expression.

"How was the chocolate?"

"Stale." Spoken with a frown.

"Seven o'clock. Don't forget."

No words. Cold stare.

When in doubt, try humor. "So, what's your favorite flower? Dead roses?"

Her lip might have twitched with the most microscopic of smiles, but it was hard to tell for sure. She turned to go.

"Seven," I called after her. "Don't forget."

"Downsized," Mr. Franka said. "What does that really mean?"

"Fired," someone said.

"Right. We use polite language to avoid words that are considered harsh or rude. *Heck* instead of *hell*. *Darn* instead of *damn*. *Put to sleep* instead of *killed*. What do we call that?"

"Euphemisms," Julia said.

"Shoot," I muttered. "I knew that."

Lunchtime. Bravery time. I knew what I had to do. I walked across to Lee's table. A couple of other girls glanced at me, then turned back to their conversations.

"I'll pick you up at seven," I said, raising my voice enough so everyone at the table would hear me. Not that any of them paid any attention to me.

I waited, hoping that Lee wouldn't shoot me down in front of everyone. Though if she did, I probably deserved it. She didn't say a word. That was fine. At least I'd made my point that I wasn't afraid to be seen with her.

· · ·

I tried to figure out how to get a ride, but I could only come up with one idea, and the very thought of it sent warning twitches through most of my internal organs.

"I need a huge favor," I said to Wesley on the way home from school.

"Name it."

"I've got a date for the dance. Can you give us a ride?"

"Sure."

"One other thing . . ." I said.

"Yeah?"

I handed him ten dollars. "Would you mind buying gas before you pick me up?"

"You got it."

"Thanks." Between Bobby and Wesley, I figured I was single-handedly supporting the petroleum industry.

May 17

I haven't been this nervous since the day school started. On top of everything else, I'm worried about getting Wesley and Lee in the same small space. There's no way to guess what they might say to each other.

It's close to seven. I'm dressed and ready. Any minute now, I expect to hear Wesley's car rumbling down the road.

For the first time in my life, I wish I'd had a ton of homework to help keep me busy. But I don't. So I did something else with my free time. I dyed my hair. It's sort of red. The folks weren't thrilled about that—Dad was already kind of annoyed because the 'vette barely made it home from work. But it felt like the right thing to do. I guess I'm making a statement. Though I'm not sure what that statement is. Maybe it's like one of those poems that doesn't really mean anything.

Even with all the time I spent making my head look like a radish, and the time I spent getting lectured about being foolish, it's still not time to leave. So here I am, having a one-sided conversation with a fetus, and hoping that Lee and Wesley don't instantly start hissing at the sight of each other.

Hey—I hear something out front, but it doesn't sound like Wesley's Mustang. It's a lot smoother. Hang on.

My God, you won't believe what's in the driveway. I have to run.

{ thirty-two }

mr. Franka taught us that most movies are broken into three acts. I guess I can do the same with my evening. So, here goes:

Act I: Driven Crazy

There was a limo in the driveway. The big kind that's stretched out so much it looks like it can't possibly turn a corner. I figured the driver had gotten lost, or someone had given him the wrong address.

When I got outside, I found Wesley waiting by the passenger side. He was wearing a long-sleeved white shirt, blue sport coat, pressed dress pants, and a chauffeur's cap. I stared at his clothes. He barely even glanced at my hair.

"What the . . . where'd you . . ."

He grinned. "Borrowed it. Slick, huh?"

All I could do was nod.

"Well, get in."

"I'll be right back." I ran to my room and grabbed the flower I'd bought. A single fresh red rose. Then I dashed back out. When I reached for the handle on the front door, Wesley shook his head. "Nope. The client rides in the rear."

It was like stepping into a small living room. The seat was more comfortable than our couch. As I was settling in, the partition behind Wesley rolled down and he said, "Where to, sir?" It looked like he was half a block away.

I gave him Lee's address. He nodded, then tapped the gas gauge. "Full up. Took a bit more than ten bucks, but I swung by the YMCA on the way here."

As we rolled off, I had visions of spending a significant chunk of my life in prison for grand theft. Though, from what I'd heard, they let convicts write books. Maybe I could even work in the prison library.

The limo barely made it around the curve in Lee's driveway. I knocked on her door, not sure whether she'd even answer it. A moment later, the door swung open. I expected Lee, or maybe one of her parents. Instead, another girl came to the entrance.

"Is Lee here?" I asked, wondering whether I'd gone to the wrong place. Maybe this was her sister.

"I'm Lee, you moron," she said.

I blinked, and there she was. She'd taken the pins out of her face, died her hair black, and put on a dress. This was Lee without the hardware.

"So you're going?"

"Duh again, Scott."

I pointed to the dress. "You didn't have to do this. Not for me."

"I know. That's why I didn't mind." She pointed to my hair. "And you didn't have to do that."

"Now you tell me." I gave her the rose.

"Thanks. I love thorns." She stepped out on the porch. It was her turn to stare.

"That was the smallest one I could find," I said. "Is white okay?"

Lee's gaze swept from the limo to me, and then back to the limo. "This is going to be a night to remember."

Wesley held the door for Lee and smiled at her. Lee smiled back. I relaxed, knowing my worst fear wasn't in danger of coming to life. There was nothing about Lee that would draw a comment from Wesley. We headed toward the school. Two blocks later, something familiar caught my eye. When it sank in what we'd just passed, I shouted, "Stop!"

"This is not the best time to change your mind," Lee said.

"No, it's not that. We gotta stop."

Wesley kept going. I realized he couldn't hear me. As Lee asked what was wrong, I fumbled for a switch and finally managed to lower the partition. "Stop!"

This time, Wesley heard me. He stopped so quickly I almost pitched into the front seat.

"Problem?" he asked.

"My parents." I pointed behind us, where the 'vette was pulled to the curb. I could see smoke pouring out from under the hood. Dad was just climbing from the driver's side. Mom was stuffed in the passenger seat.

Wesley threw the limo in reverse and we pulled up next to them.

"What's wrong?" I asked after I'd lowered the window.

Dad was only speechless for a second or two. "Your mom's in labor," he said. "We were going to the hospital."

"Hop in," I said.

"How?" Mom shouted.

Wesley and I gave Dad a hand helping Mom go from the 'vette to the limo. The instant the doors were closed, Wesley floored it. Pretty soon, we were flying down Route 22. The hospital was only a couple miles away. Which was good because I had no desire to witness the miracle of birth from a front-row seat.

"Glad to see you," Dad said.

"I can imagine." I looked at Mom. "Are you okay?"

"I'm fine," she said. Then she gasped. I felt the car speed up.

"What's wrong?" Wesley shouted.

"It's nothing," Mom said. "Normal pains. Nothing I haven't been through before. Ignore it."

Two or three seconds later, I heard a sound I couldn't ignore. A siren.

Red and blue lights flashed through the rear windshield as a police car shot up behind us. Wesley didn't stop. "Almost there," he called. He took the exit for the hospital.

We're in a stolen limo fleeing from the cops, I thought. I glanced over at Lee.

"You sure know how to treat a girl," she said. She sniffed her rose, settled back in her seat, and smiled.

Wesley pulled into the front entrance of the hospital, hitting the brakes and spinning the steering wheel hard enough to slide the limo sideways so Mom's door was close to the curb.

Mom reached over, put her hand on my head, and stroked my hair. "Every day, you amaze me. Every morning, I look at you with . . ." She paused, as if searching for the right words.

"Joyous disbelief," Dad said. It was a strangely familiar phrase.

She and Dad got out. "Want me to wait?" I called.

Mom shook her head. "No. Go enjoy your dance."

"Go ahead," Dad said. "Nothing's going to happen here for a while."

Right. Enjoy the dance. After we explain about the stolen limo. By then, Wesley had lowered his window and was talking to the policeman.

The cop smirked and said, "I should write you up, but this is just too amusing." He didn't even ask to see Wesley's license or registration. He slapped the hood of the car. "Go on, Speedy. But keep it under the limit."

"Yes, sir, Officer. I will."

As Wesley rolled onto the street, I looked behind us toward the hospital. "Relax," Lee said. "Everything will be fine. We'll come back right after the dance."

"Joyous disbelief," I muttered. Where had I heard that before? It didn't sound like something Dad would normally say. Then it hit me. Dad was quoting one of my articles. Bobby must have showed him the paper.

Act II: Facing the Music

Wesley pulled up by the gym, then opened the door for Lee. As she got out, he stared at her and frowned like he was trying to remember something. "Wait a minute . . ." He took a step back, then laughed and said, "Freaky bitch."

"What?" Lee asked.

Oh great. I wondered how badly I'd get hurt when I tackled him. Maybe, if he only broke one leg, I'd still be able to dance, as long as I leaned on Lee for support.

Wesley tapped his chest. "You were wearing that shirt, right?"

Lee nodded.

"Cool," Wesley said. "You've got style."

"You, too," Lee said.

I'd joined them by then.

"See you after the dance," Wesley said.

"Where are you going?"

He shrugged. "Figured I'd make a couple improvements to some of the files in the principal's office. Either of you need anything changed in your permanent record?"

"I'm fine," I said. "But thanks for asking."

"Me, too," Lee said.

Wesley headed off toward the front of the building.

"Isn't that part locked?" I called after him.

His voice drifted over his shoulder. "Not for long."

As we walked toward the gym, I could sense Lee slowing down. I could sense myself slowing down, too.

"I wish we could swap hair," I said.

She nodded. "Are we trying to prove something we don't need to prove?"

"I wish I knew."

The moment we walked inside, I felt a couple pairs of eyes lock onto us. Then a couple more. Then just about everyone in the place turned toward us. I wasn't sure whether they were staring at the freakier version of me, the straighter version of Lee, or the odd combination of the two of us.

"Want to dance?" I barely heard my own voice, but I guess it was loud enough since she nodded.

We started dancing. It was a fast song, and I figured I looked like a chicken that had just encountered a high-tension power line. But Lee didn't seem to mind.

When the music stopped, I noticed a lot of people were still watching us. The first one to move was Terry. He strolled over, staring down at us from somewhere beyond six feet.

"Hey, where'd you pick up the loser?"

Those would have been fighting words. Except he said them to Lee. And then he grinned at us. Which was a good thing, since tackling Terry would have been as suicidal as tackling Wesley.

Terry held out one hand. I had to jump, but I managed to give him a high five. "Hot chocolate," he said. "That was cool writing. You're a funny guy, Hudson."

When he walked away, it was as if someone had thrown a switch in everyone's brain. We were no longer interesting. People went back to dancing.

So there I was, at the last social event of the year, dancing with a great girl. A girl who wasn't afraid to be herself. And who wasn't afraid to step away from the safety of her chosen identity. I doubt there were many other kids in the gym—or anywhere else, for that matter—who had the courage to do what Lee had done.

I was still worried about Mom, but there wasn't anything I

could do right now. Soon enough, the dance would be over and I'd go back to the hospital. For the moment, I figured I'd try to keep my worries under control.

"She looks sad," Lee said when we took a break to grab a soda.

I followed her gaze and spotted Julia standing by herself near the rear exit. "Yeah, she does look sad," I said. "She broke up with Vernon the other night."

"Why don't you dance with her," Lee said.

"What?"

"Go on. No girl should stand around by herself all night, unless she likes being alone. And I don't think Julia is that sort of girl."

"She might not want to dance," I said.

"Sure she would. Besides, girls go crazy for a head of dyed hair. Even if the head itself is slightly damaged. Go dance with her, Scott."

"If you insist." I walked toward Julia. This was like one of my dreams. Except each step took a whole lot of effort, as if the gym floor had suddenly tilted forty-five degrees.

"Hi. You okay?" I asked when I reached her.

Julia gave me a sad smile. "Yeah, I'm okay."

I guess girls lie about that, too. "Dance?" I asked.

She nodded. "I'd like that."

The band started a slow song. Ohmygod. Before I could dash away and hide, Julia stepped up close, and put a hand on my shoulder and another around my back.

We danced.

Everything felt so unreal. The dance lasted a lifetime, but

ended in an eyeblink. We swayed together for a moment after the music stopped. I think she would have stayed in my arms forever. After an eternity, I let go of her and stepped back.

"Thanks," Julia said. "That was nice of you."

"My pleasure."

"And thanks for sharing your crackers with me."

"You remember that?"

"Of course." She smiled, then said, "I figured you'd forgotten all about it. I guess we kind of lost touch with each other."

"Yeah." I had to ask her something. "The other night. Why'd you say I was lucky?"

"Look at you, Scott. You've got it made."

"No, I don't."

"Are you kidding? You're on the newspaper. You were in the stage crew. You got elected to student council. Everywhere I look, there you are. I don't know how you managed to fit it all in."

"It's no big deal."

"Yes, it is. Everyone reads your articles. The jocks love the attention. You're smart. You get good grades. You live in a nice house. Your parents aren't split up or anything."

"But . . ."

"Do you have any idea how many kids would love to be you?"

No idea at all. I shrugged, hopelessly confused. My God. It was just like the stories we'd read in English. Except this wasn't some O. Henry tale with a twist ending. This was my life. My amazing life.

"There's the irony," I said.

It was her turn to be puzzled. "What do you mean?"

"Through my eyes, you're the one with the great life." As I spoke, I saw something else through my eyes. Vernon was rumbling toward us from my left. I spoke the next words quickly, both because I knew I didn't have much time, and because I needed to get them out before I lost my nerve. "You're gorgeous, Julia. You're smart. And you're wonderful. Trust me. You are very special."

Vernon pushed my shoulder. I turned to face him. I wasn't scared of him anymore. I wasn't scared of anyone. The crowd had closed in around us, sniffing at the promise of bloodshed.

"I warned you," Vernon said.

I looked right in his eyes. The first time he'd threatened me, he'd been with three of his friends. Last week, when he'd beaten me up, he'd jumped me from behind.

The truth was right in front of me. Vernon was a coward. I thought about all those hours I'd watched him on the football field. The way he ran, the way he threw the ball. His whole strategy was controlled by fear. It was in the way he wrestled, too. That's why he lost so often. Fear ruled his life.

Face-to-face, one-on-one, he wouldn't throw a punch. Not when I was free to fight back. I was dead certain of that.

Vernon glanced over his shoulder. I guess he was looking for his friends. I spotted a couple of his buddies heading toward us. They didn't make it. Ben and the rest of the stage-crew guys cut them off. A couple basketball players joined the crew. There was nobody backing Vernon up. If he wanted to start something, he'd have to do it alone and face-to-face.

"You're just a bunch of freshmen losers," he said. He glared at me, sneered at Julia, then walked off.

"Talk about a limited viewpoint," I said. "Though I don't think it's third person. More like last person."

That got another smile from Julia.

I went back to Lee. "Except for the part where it almost led to my death, that wasn't such a bad suggestion."

"I thought so."

The band played another slow song.

I opened my arms and Lee stepped toward me as if we'd done this a million times.

"So, who do you like dancing with better?" she asked, resting her head against my shoulder.

"That's not the sort of question I'd expect from you," I said.

"People change," she said.

"Yeah. Everything changes. Flux is all around us." *Who did I like dancing with better?* I held her a bit closer. "No contest, Lee."

Act III: Oh Brother

"Where'd you get the limo?" I asked Wesley as we headed back to the hospital. We were all riding in the front now.

"Told you already," he said. "I borrowed it."

"Yeah, but who'd you borrow it from?"

He pointed at a small sign on the dashboard next to the glove compartment. *Wesco Limos.* I leaned closer. *Wesley Cobble Sr., Owner.*

"Your dad owns Wesco Limos?" I asked.

He nodded. "Rents snowmobiles, too. And Jet Skis." He hit the brakes and turned to stare at me. "You think I steal cars?"

"Of course not."

Wesley nodded and drove on. "I've been tempted a couple times."

"Please don't," I said.

"Yeah, please don't," Lee said. "We'd hate to see you get sent away." She turned to me. "Speaking of which, you know what?"

"What?" I put my arm around her. She didn't seem to mind.

"You keep insisting you were nice to Mouth even though you didn't like him."

"Yeah."

"But I'm pretty sure you're lying to yourself."

"No way. Guys never lie."

"Yeah, right. The thing is, I think you sort of liked Mouth all along."

I'd never imagined that possibility. But then again, I never imagined I'd be dancing with Lee. Maybe I did sort of like Mouth. I was still writing to him. I guess that meant something. And I was always thinking about the wild stuff he'd said.

Wesley pulled back onto Route 22. This time, he kept the limo within ten miles of the limit. At least, for most of the trip. "I'll wait here," he said when we reached the hospital. "Take your time."

"No, you won't." I opened the door and slid out. "I want you to come. Both of you."

So there we were. Me and Lee and Wesley, standing on one side of a big glass window, gazing at my new brother. He stared right back at me, too. Like he already knew he could trust me.

"He looks just like you," Lee said to me.

"Nah," Wesley said. "He's a lot less goofy."

"If that's what I look like," I said, "just kill me now."

Dad came up behind me and put an arm around my shoulders. "Life is good," he said.

"Nwarries, might," I said.

"What?" Dad asked.

"Oh, just something I learned in Spanish," I told him. Then I introduced him to my friends.

Wow. Two small words that mean a lot. *My friends.*

Still May 17

Happy birthday.

Sorry I don't have a present for you, but you showed up a bit early. Not that I would have had something if you were on time. Wait, I do have something for you. I have a promise.

I won't let you down. Honest. I might make your life miserable, and play the most awful tricks on you, and exploit you in every conceivable way, but I swear I'll never let you down.

For example—I won't lie to you. I'll tell you right now, newborn babies are ugly. Possibly even hideous. Every single one. You're no exception. Ick. Just thought you'd want to know.

I'm not even all that jealous. Except for one thing. You get to sleep as much as you want. I'd do anything to trade places. Well, anything except wear a diaper.

I guess that's about it for this thing I've been writing, whatever it is. I may make a few more notes now and then, but I think all the tips and stuff I put here should be enough to give you a good start. You can avoid my mistakes and make some of your own. That's what life is all about.

Welcome to my world, Sean. You ugly toad.

{ thirty-three }

I put the notebook away for a while. But I couldn't get out of the habit of writing. So I tried other things. Stories. Plays. Even some poems, though I'd never admit that to anyone except Lee. And Mr. Franka.

I've been writing letters, too. Mostly to Mouth. He writes back. Long rambling letters. But it's not just noise. He has a lot to say. So do I. Some of which I'll share with the world. And some of which I'll save for a special audience.

June 7

I'm home. School's over. I figured the last day deserved an entry. Not that this is a diary. I can't take too long, because Wesley and Lee are waiting for me downstairs. We're going out for pizza. Lee's gotten good at keeping Wesley from stealing knives and saltshakers. Though she somehow got her hands on that guillotine last week, so I suspect she doesn't object to everything Wesley does.

From now on, I can tell you stuff in person. Even if you're currently pretending not to understand a word I say. Actually, with all the weird sounds you're making, I think I can get you a job at Zenger teaching Spanish. *Bwaaadios.*

Mom and Dad spend a ton of time with you. Yet, paradoxically (hey—you didn't think the vocabulary words would stop just because school is out, did you?), they seem to have more time than ever for me. Dad and I are going away next weekend to do some bass fishing on Lake Erie. I'd bring you along, but we're not planning to use live bait.

I was going to buy you your first book right after you were born, but Mom beat me to it. She actually bought you six books, including *Goodnight Moon* and *pat the bunny.* It was a pretty good selection, though I would have added something a bit edgier to the mix, like *Dracula.* Or at least *Bunnicula.*

Dad bought you a plastic tool set. Maybe you'll be an all-around sort of guy. Someone who can rebuild an engine and write a sonnet. Hey, the world needs both. Engines and sonnets. They both take us places we'd never reach on our own.

Bobby called last night from New Orleans. They're about midway through the concert tour. When he got his first check, he bought us a computer. You aren't allowed near it until you get control over that whole drooling problem of yours. He and Mom talk a lot on the phone. I think he's been telling her all sorts of stuff he'd kept locked up.

I found out there's a place at the community college

that helps people who have reading problems. I didn't mention it to Bobby yet. That can wait until he comes home between tours. But he's going to find out how much pleasure there is in reading. No way I'm going to let one of my brothers miss out on that.

Julia started dating a nicer guy. I'm happy for her. We always say hi when we pass each other in the halls. Lee dyed her hair orange. It looks pretty hot. My own red disaster is growing out. I thought about shaving my head, but decided to let things go back to normal on their own schedule. It's just hair. No big deal.

They're shouting for me to come down. I really have to go. We need to celebrate the end of school. Wesley is going to graduate. And, wow, I'm not a freshman anymore. I'm a sophomore. Imagine that.

"Flux rox," Scott said, conclusively.